"Stark and insouciant, dry-witted and desperately honest, Gordon's memorable first novel mixes reflections on body, mind, illness, and soul with far-flung adventures in youth culture." —*Publishers Weekly*

"The primary ingredient to a winning novel is an incredible story. The second is excellent writing within that story. Fran Gordon's *Paisley Girl* succeeds in delivering both. Gordon's writing is so consistently poetic and insightful one can't help but reread certain metaphors and clever similes for aesthetics. This book is beautiful . . . . This novel is a masterpiece." —*Rapport*

"Witty and rich." —*Seventeen*

"An exquisitely written portrayal of being, illness, and identity. A poetic, moving book." —Lucy Grealy, author of *Autobiography of a Face* and *As Seen on TV: Provocations*

"A jaggedly sharp novel of despair and redemption . . . Gordon makes her inner torment explicit in the ravages of her illness; when she displays the progression of her protagonist's physical decay, Gordon also depicts the inner struggle of a woman who refuses to accept the soulless sterility of the life she has been leading. The well-written, fast-paced novel is heavily laced with self-aware cynicism that occasionally veers into hopefulness in spite of itself." —*Booklist*

"A gritty, hypnotic debut tale told by a perceptive young woman . . . in a voice that is variously wry, rough, fragmented, and lovely. Chaos is, in fact, the opening and closing note of this mesmerizing dream, leaving readers to mull over the intriguing parallels between start and end." —*Kirkus Reviews*

"Through rich language and imagery so real and so jarring that it makes one gasp, Gordon takes readers into Paisley's painful experience. The story reaches its conclusion as Paisley comes to terms with her disease, with life and death, and most importantly, with herself." —*Library Journal*

"*Paisley Girl* is the most lush, riveting, extreme, and inspiring novel I've read in years. Fran Gordon writes like Virginia Woolf in the grips of a terminal meth binge."
—Jerry Stahl, author of *Permanent Midnight* and *Perv: A Love Story*

"*Paisley Girl* is a story of an extraordinary stigma suffered and overcome. Written with passion and humor and raging widely across the globe, it is a haunting, beautiful, and utterly original novel."
—Patrick McGrath, author of *Asylum* and *Dr. Haggard's Disease*

"You'll find yourself reading with one hand over your mouth in astonishment at the beauty of this book as you are drawn into a strange universe of hospitals, syringes, rock stars, travel, intrigue, sex, and disease. Too erotically alive to be cynical, too searingly passionate for apolitical apathy, *Paisley Girl* takes the numbed soul of an anesthetized culture and demands that we feel again."
—Sapphire

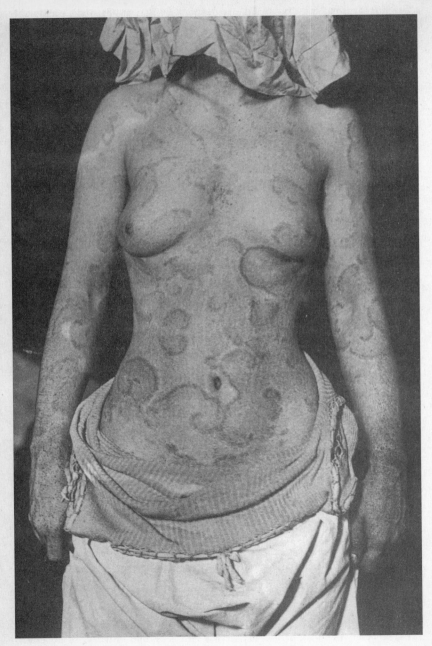

"Paisley Girl," courtesy Stanley B. Burns, M.D., and the Burns Archive

Paisley Girl

A Novel

❧

Fran Gordon

THOMAS DUNNE BOOKS
ST. MARTIN'S GRIFFIN
NEW YORK

This book is a novel. Names, characters, places, and incidents are either products of the author's imagination or are used fictitiously. Any resemblance to locales or persons, living or dead, is coincidental.

THOMAS DUNNE BOOKS.
An imprint of St. Martin's Press.

Design by Nancy Resnick

www.stmartins.com

Library of Congress Cataloging-in-Publication Data

Gordon, Fran.
    Paisley girl : a novel / Fran Gordon.
        p.   cm.
    ISBN 0-312-20352-7 (hc)
    ISBN 0-312-26371-6 (pbk)
    I. Title.
PS3557.0663P35   1999
813'.54—dc21   99-33989
                                                                  CIP

First St. Martin's Griffin Edition: October 2000

10 9 8 7 6 5 4 3 2 1

To Richard Haden Gordon III
for Dick

Paisley Girl

Paisley, the abstract figure that will in illness swathe me, mimics the shape of a fractal—or vice versa. A fractal is an illustration of the world's regular irregularity. The twist of a shoreline, the swirl of city litter. It's the confusion that develops in the human heart—the prime cause of sudden unexplained death—that confounds doctors. Yet it's always recognizable patterns. Models of chaos. Though the forms may differ vastly one from another, they have in common their self-similarity—this being the endless reflection that confronts you, should you find yourself wedged between mirrors. Or following a snail, as he navigates each pebble of a recursive coast. And because in such images, as seemingly in paisley, an endless line surrounds a finite area—in the mind's eye, these patterns are a way of seeing infinity.

Word has spread of my body, painted in the grotesque but of a shape more pleasing than that of any cafeteria-fed college girl. The students come in ever-increasing numbers. They're just starting out, and have yet to experience the endless cadavers that will numb them to flesh. I make eye contact and the cadets, all male, blush with a heady mix of lust and revulsion. They're back to their boyhood, caught in the bathroom with their father's medical journals. I shiver from stainless steel and observation, nipples hard as gravel. My breasts, as if worth sparing, have remained free of marks. I hold arms close to my sides to cheat them of these dadaist grottos, focus on the face of a freckled boy, and offer him my own. The dim purpling and slight swelling around my lips and eyes make me look beaten. I've noticed that this elicits sympathy from women, while men are reminded of some sagittary within that they don't like being made aware of. The boy quickly averts his gaze to study instead the linoleum that peels up from the floor. There is rot beneath the shiny surface. An ambush of decay. The blood doctor, bland as rice, asks if I'd like to come downstairs later to a staff cocktail party—"guest-of-honor," he adds, matter-of-factly. I'm too weak to decline verbally, so I offer my eyes as response. He sees in them the threat that they will hold his image indefinitely.

"Paisley Girl" is how they see me, what they call me, though never to my face. Pity. I prefer it to the slam of "sweetie," "darlin'" or when they err, when I ache—"champ." I am not the aloud but what is whispered. Paisley: it's my *nom de grrl*. The shape of my marks. Abstract, infinite. *Unnatural as woman*. And while the doctors look to delineate causes—I see chaos. The geometry between dimensions. Steroids keep me in this interstice; each day I am injected and embalmed.

I'm stuck, but if God is in the spaces in between, then mine has fallen, like a much-needed sock, or a grandmother's earring, behind an empty bureau that I'm too weak to move.

The walls are whitest at four—forlorn hour before dawn, intemperate hour of burnt fury. Hour of little blue light batting zero. It's then my angel appears, blue as the blink of that clock come unplugged—and stinking, like vomit. His blue is regulation, the vomit varies. This time it's from the post-op next door, I can tell by the chemical smell—though he could just as well have been doused with the contentless bile of chemo, an old man's urine, or the tsunamied sea of a preemie. I call him Gil, because he breathes so easily beneath the stench of so many fluids. He calls me Paisley. Aloud.

"Oh man Gil, you smell," I say. "Light a match," and

he does. It's our ritual, my only relief. He smiles and re-moves a joint from the only pocket sewn for orderlies, the one atop his heart. He lights peppermint paper, burns a sweet-smell, kneels beside my prostrate body.

"The docs treating you all right?"

"They're treating me, all right. Domo even invited me to a staff cocktail party as the 'guest of honor,' but I wasn't sure I could take all that publicity."

"You mean to tell me you missed hapless hour? I bet the elevators were going full blast."

"Well, I'm sure it was a fête, but I hadn't a thing to wear, what with my tea-length paper gown still at the cleaners and all."

"You keep this up, P., and you'll never make Miss World."

"Oh well—that's life," I say, and smoke it down, while, beside me, he lights up again.

"How about you—what did they remove from the 'living sac' this time?" I ask.

"Sutures they left in the last. I may have to cut out quick if I hear him start up again, don't want him to choke himself. No sir, that wouldn't be right; he's just a piano teacher, not a rock star."

"Janis Joplin is alive and living with a fireman," I say, and think of lives cut short by their own reflex.

"What? Who told you that?"

"Read it."

"Musta dreamt it, P."

"Last night I had a dream I was outside, first thing I did was to get a good, strong cup of coffee. The cheapest is best, you know, all arabica beans, so I went into Burger

King. A boy named Kurt Cobain was working there. He was happy."

"Paisley, you're crazy. C'mon now, gimme some." Then, under his breath, he says, "Bogart."

"The sac must have been happy to see you—Betty," I say and relinquish the weed.

"Oh they never *see* me, and if they do, they don't remember," he says, flicking thanklessness like a lost ladybird. "That juice you can't have does it to them." He calls anaesthetics and painkillers "this juice" or "that juice." "I'm just a dream that maybe it's best they forget."

"Not so."

"Is so."

"So—am I dying?"

"Girl, you ain't dying . . . girl you're *nowhere*," he answers between tokes, then passes me the spliff. "Let's roam," he says.

Dreams are mine to keep, and Gil, a man who pulls socks full of toes off feet too decomposed to wash, is my wide-awake favorite. He's unfazed by paisley.

"Disease," he says. "Ain't nothin' so ordinary."

"But, my marks," I say.

"Marks is marks," he answers. He thinks mine decorative.

When the night is heaviest, I wink at him. He holds my hand, says, "So how do *you* think you're doing?"

"All is well."

"You been reading Testiclees again?"

"*Soph*ocles," I smile, "and I gave that book to you."

"I know."

"I feel better now."

"Yeah, well, I see you fixing on some far point—you stay put, hear?"

I hear. An emptied man gags and my dream disperses. He drops the roach in his half-full cup, sprays Lysol.

"Whoops, gotta go clear his blowhole, 'night, P."

" 'Night, Gil."

But there's no night, only dawn. No dark hole of forgotten dream to slough my soul into. I'm tired. So tired. But the pain's gone—for now. I still can't lie on my back, though; they take from what is left, and what is left is woman, just enough round to dig bone-deep down and gauge samples of cells that continue to have the children these hips will not. I lie on my stomach, elbows up, window out of view—face to the cellblock, back to the door.

They've quick-frozen enough parts of me, unwell and brilliant with color, to be sent thrice round the world for scrutiny. They pluck plugs of tissue like gold rings of the unknown. I feel their rushed sewing with thick thread. I guess they're careless because corpses needn't worry about scars. I know they rush because the local's cocaine, a brief holdover. It's all my blood can tolerate. No more generals, not since the last one.

Domo counted backward. "Ten, nine, eight . . ." *Hutt*. My heart locked; my throat closed. Beyond arrhythmia, beside myself, I saw boxes wheeled in, their light morbid with bones of radium. Churlish hands, stinking of ions and old batteries, rub themselves together before grabbing me back. The doctors, in a panic over the possibility of prosecution, work furtively until a malevolent helpmate appears, a glassy-eyed nurse with needle extended. She's amped for her swing shift—pitched, impatient, and underpaid. She grinds her teeth, seizes the chart from the bed like a spent casing, and lights a cigarette. I look up, scared and suffocated. I'd like a drag.

"Don't move," she warns. I close my eyes and await relief; I envision a narcotic plunge but am given instead the subcutaneous sting of adrenalin that shakes and slaps me awake. "Lie still; stay *down!*" Her words come diamond, her inflection a drill. *Down.* Through murk, flesh, red—a second strike. The jolt jars my arm. The room is pulsing. My heart is pounding, in protest, in excess, but I am where I am, in America, in illness where stitches become slipshod and dosages increase like darkness in autumn.

We're losing the light.

And though my heart races, my words come Valium, stupefying and senseless. The nurse checks my pulse, passably erratic, and sips from the Coca-Cola that I suspect has been her only sustenance for hours, days, a life of a red-spattered white. Then she turns her junk-eaten face away and floats down the hall to save her next victim, all the while muttering a mantra of departure between abraded teeth, "Stupid guys, stupid girl, stupid world."

Studies continue sans anaesthesia. The cocaine solution never lasts longer than twenty minutes—about the time it takes for the ice in Doc's post-op highball to melt—then pain comes screaming like a car crash.

More and more they call me "champ."

Perversion persists, and, as if to ensure total humiliation, they put me in pediatrics. I take this designation as license. I yell. I curse. I make up games. I encourage children to summon nurses with their call button to ask them riddles. We call this game Sphinx. They all like to play, but most mispronounce it (they have little preciosity—and far too much knowledge). When a nurse arrives to find no one's end in sight, she chokes back her own rage and wags a finger at me. I tell her to fuck off, then turn to Austin, the child closest to me. "It's not polite to point. Is it?" he asks.

"No," I say. His mother's boyfriend has had the bad manners to pummel him again until his brain inflated past the puff of prior beatings. Austin, just three, has come out of his seventh operation. This time they've put a steel plate into his head. "To let your thoughts flow clearly," I say. The rim juts from his forehead, facing the world like wisdom withheld them.

Austin is a good boy. He likes soft things.

Charlie plays "Taps" on Austin's head. "*Stop it*—please," I say. The kids look at me with concern. They think it's a march. Charlie, a bruiser full of bad blood, drops the toy xylophone sticks, red, white, and blue, and Austin stops humming. "Doesn't that hurt?" I ask him.

"No," he says, and hugs the rag doll beside him.

"Well . . . you both should be resting."

"I'm sorry I woke you," says Austin. I want to say, no,

that I was awake all along—but I can't. He'd know I was lying. He knows too much. Instead I say, "I was dreaming about heaven."

"Where the fishes are?" says Austin, excitedly.

"Yes," I say, "where the fishes are."

The last time Austin was home his dog died. Whether from the boot or old age remains unclear. He told me his mother (herself a child) had said that the dog was going to heaven, and not to cry. He didn't. And when they brought the body to a local pet store that offered to dispose of it, Austin was happy his dog had been taken to heaven. But he'd never expected that there were so many fishes there—gold and striped and orange and fringed.

Before the boys woke me I'd been dreaming about heaven. So many dead children amongst so much fish. I'd found them when—like at swim practice when I'd been too weak to butterfly—I dove down to travel submerged in dream. Somehow, I made it to the deep end, where one could tread and tread in water of a still and silent blue. I felt nice there—but then a whistle sounded, and an effeminate voice said, "Get out of the water." I looked up and saw that it was Frankie Avalon.

"Why?" I asked.

"Because you're not a kid," he said.

"Oh," I said.

"You missed that boat."

"Yes. I know." I was no longer a child and yet I'd not surpassed the age white cells could grow past control. Kids get leukemia—well, kids and Charles Bukowski—perhaps I'd remained stunted.

"Why the fuck is breakfast so late?!" I say when I see the nurse.

"Stop it, you'll scare the children!" she says. But I don't—they just smirk—they know they've got an out.

Still, they'd rather go home.

I left home at seventeen, the last year of my wellness. Of girlhood. Reagan was president; kids dressed like duck hunters and aimed for status quo. My friend Willa and I'd yearned to travel. We wanted to get past America. We wanted the world. No one else did. At the hostage crisis pep rally, preppies pelted an Ayatollah effigy with tennis balls while Willa and I pogoed to the Clash on the bus ramp. While everyone listened to Foreigner, Willa and I wandered. Hers was the first house in town to have cable. We watched *My Fair Lady* and MTV. We were punk aristocrats; we got stoned, sipped tea, and spoke in fractured accents. Sometimes we sang: "Stand Down Margaret" or "Ça Plane Pour Moi"—but never "99 Luftballoons." We were fools for euphony, all Brits seemed like barons. One day we skipped class to see Stevie Winwood. It was Winwood I'd wanted. But it was Crash that I caught.

By the time Willa and I arrived at the concert, Stevie was playing oldies. I'd missed "Higher Love." And to make matters worse, Cultural Exhaust, the opening act, the band all the art students at school were raving about, had already played.

Backstage after the show, I played. My game was called "stare." I thought that if I focused long and hard enough on the object of my attention, he'd turn around. But Winwood was gone, so I focused on a roadie. He turned around, and smiled at Willa. "I'm Rafe," he said.

"*Rafe?*"

"Yes?"

"I'm outta here," she said, then corrected herself. "I'm outta weed."

"Well, *you* smoked it all," I said.

"Bad traffic, good weed—what do you want from me?"

"Damn, Willa!"

"What?"

I just shook my head. She'd blown our cover. Now Rafe knew we were old enough to drive, knew there was no mom waiting by the curb. I'd gotten us out of backstage parties this way, panties intact. We'd puffed with UB40, and ate dinner with B. B. King. We even met Elvis Costello before he'd abstained—along with Nick Lowe. Old Nick posed some danger. But when I said, "Tonight's my birthday—I'm fifteen!" we were coddled and sent home with pats on the head. Miraculously, my ploy had always worked. I tried using "sixteen" once, but that was just fuel on the fire. *Fifteen forever, friends for life*, this was our motto. I'd lived for experience, a bimbo-Blake, but Willa and me were mostly innocent.

"Oh—*Ralph!*" she said. His name was sewn in small letters on his jacket, the back of which was emblazoned with Cultural Exhaust.

"Oh Willa." He reached into his pocket. By the look on his face, I expected him to present her with a ring, but instead he offered us a McDonald's spoon and a film canister. I reached but she grabbed my hand.

"Take a picture, it'll last longer." Willa didn't do coke. "One addiction is enough," she'd always said. Me—I just wanted more.

Ralph led the way.

Stevie was a dear—but stoned out of his mind. And his wife, a blond American, was eight months pregnant. Someone had given her the life-size stuffed gorilla to whom he spoke seriously. The gorilla was larger than Stevie. I just loved pint-size prodigies. It was a pity he was taken—a pity he was gone. I wondered if he stopped growing after "Gimmie Some Lovin'." He'd been thirteen when he wrote it. That made him forty-three. Wow. A geezer. Maybe if I'd done my math, I'd have wasted less time fantasizing about Stevie taking me far away. As it turned out, he lived in Nashville.

Willa saw Stevie's pipe and joined him and his monkey. She sat on the gift as if it was Santa. Ralph gave me the blow. "Go on, be *bad*," he said, and followed my friend. I'd have to drive, so I pocketed the blow, and loaded a plate full of pasta—no use getting busted. Just then I noticed a boy I hadn't seen before. He had the most arresting red hair. Pale skin but no freckles. He looked young. And he was tall, very tall. Gangly. He wore a long coat, so it was hard to tell exactly how thin he was. He was alone. He'd been following me. Skulking down the hallway. *Staring*. Did he know me? His eyes—*good god his eyes*—were green. His lashes, red and long. (It's always the boys.) I didn't see then that no matter the joy, he'd always look as if he'd been crying.

I stepped closer. Carelessly toward color. I knew this was fate, but didn't realize its purpose is to prod—not sustain. "Hungry?" the boy said, and eyed my plate.

This is how I first desired Crash—young, sad, famished, unfamous. It's how I'll always desire him. "You're brilliant," he said. Like it was my name. I was mystified. Willa was the goddess—I was just a nymph. When I realized envy had been the motive behind so many seemingly random acts of cruelty, I sought stunning friends. I'd rather feel plain than pain.

"You're beautiful." I'd never said that to a boy before. He seemed as stunned as me.

"No," he said, "I'm Crash."

I laughed.

"See now—I'm funny-looking."

"Where did 'Crash' come from?"

"The Isle of Wight—where everyone's inbred. That's why I'm funny-looking."

I smile, I'm hooked. "That's not what I meant."

"My name then?"

I nodded.

"I've wrecked a few cars—and bought some already smashed. I go for bangers, collect American."

Ralph approached. "She doesn't look American."

Crash stammered and lit a Dunhill.

"May I?"

"Sorry? Oh." Reluctantly, he gave me a cigarette. He was either very cheap—or sweet. "So then, what do you do?"

"Go to school."

"Are you smart?" He liked this—that I was smart. "I stopped lessons at sixteen."

"A few years ago?" I say.

Crash laughs. "A lifetime, luv. A lifetime."

Within minutes, I'd forgotten Willa. Crash snuck me across the street to his hotel room. Up close, he wasn't as young as I'd thought. He told me he was thirty-three. His chest, though, was bare as a boy's. He was a wraith. The red, however, was real—and his cock was huge, bigger around than my wrist, bigger than us both. Like there was three of us there. He seemed to be staving someone off. His callused fingers fluttered across my flesh. I wasn't sure whether it was alarm or desire I felt at these hands. He nibbled me anxiously. Like a piece of cake he was trying hard not to devour. So, was I poison—or a ration for life? I felt put upon by this fuss, part of me wanted to remain intact, unruffled. But—as a woman guides a fitful child to the breast he can't see—I slipped off my skirt and guided Crash inside.

"Shit, stupid, sor-eeee," he said. And came. The pressure on us both was released.

My ache had begun.

I lit two of his cigarettes in silence. "I've never slept with a man on the first night," I said. He held me tight, all ribs and knobs.

"You shouldn't . . . smoke."

"Were you *bad* then?" Ralph said, when I returned.

"Maybe. Don't know. I'm not sure." I dug in my pocket, gave him the coke.

He popped the top. "Ah—a good girl then. *Dommage.* Your friend certainly overindulged." Willa nodded on the

couch. "The boss's Mrs. was kind enough to keep these."
He handed me the car keys.

"Thanks, Ralph, thanks a lot."

"I can't believe you left me at the circus," Willa said,
when I nudged her.

"What?"

"With the midget and his monkey."

"That was Winwood."

"Sherwood?" she slurred. "Here try some of this pot."

I took a hit. "Damn, this is strong." I took another.
"Well no wonder you're whacked—this shit is . . ."

"Opium," said Ralph.

I slumped in the couch, stared at the ceiling fan.

"Oh God," said Willa. "We're goners."

"Speak for yourself," I said.

The next day my dorm reeked of flowers, a thousand unbud, courtesy of Crash.

And a ticket to London. Soon I'd be as far away as I
wanted.

Home is horizon. Other patients are sent to theirs, canceled insurance slips in hand; I'm switched from the kids back to my single. I stew in memories, stare at the tube.

"You watching the fight?" Gil says.

It hasn't begun. "What are you doing here so early? It's daylight, Gil, won't you melt or something?"

"Yeah, or something," he yawns. "I come to watch a little . . ." he says, and looks up at the screen. "Damn, you watching *60 Minutes* again?"

"It's not your shift, Gil."

"Girl, don't you know I swing?" he says sly.

"You never used to," I say, and turn my back, half-heartedly.

"Yeah, well they're sticking it to me now. I think someone told them about our soirées."

"They're just jealous they're not invited," I say, but Gil's attention is on the tube.

"Damn. Why don't they send someone besides Ed Bradley into the ghetto?" he says. I shrug; I have trouble finding an answer that's not part of the problem.

"You know Ed Bradley goes fishing with Hunter Thompson," I say.

"P., you're a cornucopia of related disparities," says Gil.

"Whoa professor—what's with the words?"

"Guess I've been reading too many books from the nineteenth century. Hey—they're the only things on the carts besides *Good Housekeeping* and outdated copies of *Time*." At this, I bend to look beneath the bed but am unable to get back up. Gil lifts me like it was nothing, as if I was a page blown from a sun-dappled desk. Then he looks below, and sees what I was after. "*The Magic Mountain*. You read this?"

"Not yet."

"Man, these words'll take forever."

"Take it—I don't like the idea of you reading outdated *Time*; it depresses me," I say.

"No reason, P., last month's news is just next year's—or the next. See, I'm ahead of the game."

"What about change?" I say.

"Change is soon spent, P., we just sit and watch the world go round."

"What time is it?" I ask.

"Why?" he says.

"I want to know how much of the show's left."

"P., don't start to worry about time now—just stay hung up on words, okay? Time's a secret that ain't worth knowing."

"You know at the end of *60 Minutes*, when time runs out?"

"You mean right before that moron, Rooney," says Gil.

"Yes, well, I want the tv to explode then, when the clock's done, but it doesn't. It just keeps going."

"Clock don't keep going. I know cause I'm watching—when Rooney's done I turn the mute button off."

"No. The tv keeps going. When the show's over, everyone who's been watching Ed or cursing Andy, well, they're on to the next cast. Within minutes of that clock ticking down, they're all thinking of something other than *60 Minutes*. *60 Minutes*'s time has passed. It's over. Done."

"And you have a problem with that?" says Gil.

"It scares the shit out of me," I say.

"P., you ain't had no shit come out of you for weeks."

"Bet she ain't either," I say, as the nurse creeps past my door to her bathroom.

"What? She *lives* in the crapper."

"C'mon, Gil, you know she goes there to shoot, not shit."

"Mmm. Guess I'm a little tight myself with the schedule they got me on. I think they're looking to get rid of me, P."

"No way Gil, you're the best."

"They're cutting back."

"Not the best."

"They sacked my friend Oliver uptown."

"Maybe he had it coming," I say, though I know better.

"No, that man ain't had nothing coming but a Nobel. Things change in an instant, P. *BANG*."

"Just like that."

"Just like that," Gil says. Then he's gone.

Crash had begun to disappear. When my illness flared, he was gone.

I remember how he'd lain his head in my lap like an offering. A rite for life. Or so I thought. Even when his locks snarled, unkempt and uncut. And his habits began to scare me. Still, I ran my hands through his blaze, grateful for length.

Of all the colors, red has the least range. But it catches the eye like a virus.

I checked out of London without seeking treatment. And committed myself to the anti-socialized medicine of the States. The first doctor I consulted gave me antifungals—which I found out cause birth defects for up to three years after use (not that I'll have these lambs, or those three years). He injected me with antihistamines, antibiotics, anti-this, anti-that. "Ante up," he said. And I rolled my sleeves. Two of the drugs used in combination cause anti-life. I learned this on the news. There was a rash of athlete's foot sufferers who had hay fever that season; then there were less—less men, less mowed lawns—more hay fever. . . . I stopped taking the antifungal. Pain bloomed.

But the doctor refused to prescribe anything else. "You're on too much medication," he said. He didn't say why. When I admitted I didn't take all the meds, he looked at me as if I'd missed curfew. I grasped for explanations and alibis. "I think I'm allergic," I said.

The next day he crosshatched my back with a dime-store ballpoint, then stuck a hundred needles in. The bill was thousands more. I'm allergic to nothing.

"Maybe I have what's going around," I said to the next doctor.

"What's going around? Hay fever?"

"AIDS."

"You're just a girl," he said, and ran every test, except the one I requested. So I turned to Public Health. I walked into a gray-green pile that could have passed for one of Stalin's halls, except that neither the building nor the children inside were being maintained. The women there had soured, their babies, so many, were wrapped and red, like sick sausages. The men were angry, and insubstantial as condiments. I was given a number. When it was up I was sent to another waiting room, full of junkies and whores. Not the movie kind—not the ones full of verve, too thin but beautiful, with breasts like mine, round and unmarred. No. The breasts before me were sad, slumped. Some had scratches. Most of the girls gazed without focus. A few glared. I bowed my head ashamed— next to them, I looked beatific. Then a voice bellowed. My number was up, again. I faced the nurse, rolled my sleeves. "Ante up," I said. She looked from the tracks they'd lain to the immobility of my face—and sighing, she struck.

The next week, I returned.

My number wasn't called, instead I was motioned into an office papered with posters that urged protection against love, precaution against pregnancy. "Multiple partners?" the counselor said, as if proffering a cigarette.

"No. No thanks."

"Your boyfriend . . . Did he have many partners?"

"No. None at all."

"Did he *sleep around?*"

"Don't know," I said. "Don't think so."

"Did he shoot dope?"

"He did," I said, glad to have a straight answer.

"Does he still?"

"Don't know."

"He should drop by."

"He should," I said.

"You should send him."

"Can't. Don't know where he is."

"You don't know much about him, huh?"

"No. Not anymore."

She looked at my arms, their paisley. "I don't know what that is, but this test's negative. You have the chance these people don't," she says, then looks closer at the clotted bruises near my needle marks. "You don't use?" she said.

"They're from the doctors."

"For what?"

"Tests, treatment."

"Lord, they should spend a second or so on technique. Look, I'm sorry you're sick. Wish there was . . . Are you a runaway?" she asked, then answered herself. "No, you're too soft to be street."

"Like quicksand," I said, and slipped further into silence, while my cells continued to lay upon the landscape of my body a cartography of chance—sinistral, aeonian, fathomless.

The woman you listed on the admissions form doesn't exist."

"You caught me. Does this mean I won't graduate with honors?"

Domo clears his throat. "Your next of kin is not 'Mrs. Rouault.' *Who* is your next of kin?"

"What does it matter? What do you want?"

"It's not what I want—it's what you need."

"A hole in my head?"

"Bone marrow."

"Oh," I say. "Is that a fact?"

The doctors still know nothing about my disease, so they treat it as if it's another—one they can cure. They give me chemotherapy. But not "aggressively," they say, as if poison can't be passive. They give me interferon. Only a certain amount of both is allowed per lifetime, so with each execution I feel mine slide further, like mud from the rains on a brushfired mountain. There's hair on my pillow— payment from some poor fairy, now bald. I'm not yet. Last night, I dreamt that my skull was covered with what looked to be black chick fuzz. The first thing I thought was how bad the new short cut would look on me. Then I realized this wasn't a dream on the ephemera of fashion, but on how I might look upon entering eternity.

Light falls fitful now in my rough white room. Sparrows pass pane and school toward my bed. They squash like rotten fruit when I swat them. My thumb stuck through one comes up bloody. I awake shamed to find it sucked. Between bitten blistered lips. And on my skin, handprints where I've hit.

Only the mind's child survives bodily schism. This is how I live: not intact, but attached.

One out of ten marrow transplants ends in death. I suspect that, as usual, I'll be in the minority. I know that no amount of pain on my part can spare another theirs. I know I must decline. I'll keep my chances—the ones I have that others do not. Still, to appease principals, I go through preliminaries. Squeeze statistics from oncologists and bring up experimental odds, lighter than bird bones.

∽

She said *no?*" says the intern.

"*I* said no."

"What are the chances of that?"

"Survival?" says Domo.

"Refusal," says the intern.

"Scant. At least we can use her to map aerophagia in allergic response; this way we can bypass PETA problems." Domo tries using his language to mute me.

"Allergic to her own blood—how unusual."

"What do you mean *allergic?* I'm not allergic to anything."

"She has too many mast cells," says Domo.

"Funny," I say, "how poor my reception is here."

But they don't get it.

They say that my mast cells, white and weighty, assail as if my body, my blood is disease. They say this is rare—but I'm not so sure. "Mast cells are immune cells that release histamines. . . ." says Domo.

". . . ammo for the bod, in fight-or-flight snafus—like allergies," says a student.

"Histines are released in labor," says another.

"I was born on Labor Day," I say.

The students break for a moment to consider this—that I was once as new and stainless as the metals hung round their necks.

"Skin is an organ, so . . ."

". . . so mine plays acid jazz."

"You're something else."

"My immune system thinks I'm something else too—and it's killing me."

Domo clicks his pen. As if to call order.

"Mast cells also release pigment, thus her pyrotechnics," he says.

"My brother was born on the Fourth of July," I say. "Mom liked to avoid celebrations."

"You have a brother?"

"No, nevermind," I say. And they don't.

In England, my birthday fell on Fire Day. A year ago, Crash and I'd spent it at Covent Garden. I looked toward the opera house and swore I heard Callas scream beauty. But it had just been a cry from the child behind me. I sweated sumptuously, sifted deep beneath a ruin of silk I'd found, and draped myself before a mirror streaked with age. Although my robes were stiff as if from the smear of some primordial gluten, I imagined them soft, imagined I was an abbess, a Borgia, an astrologer that could divine all but the £1000 price tag upon my illusion.

Crash stood in front of the marcasite booth, looking for an asp.

When he couldn't find one, he settled for a salamander. Slashed the pin through unbought silk and held a palm beneath to shield my precious flesh. The glitter of tail was suspect, more golden than the requisite gray. A fake fake of a snake. Too toy to age well. "It's brilliant," I said.

Crash loved me for my lucent skin and I accepted his knighthood, wide-eyed. I loved him for his love. His beauty and his blues. He paid for it all. "Too much," I'd said, abashed. But continued to buy.

We liked markets. I for possibility—he for the chance to kill time. Now, the ending in his behavior aggrieves me. And the memory of Crash crushes me with conclusion: He'd acted on things to stifle the impulse from whence they came. He drank to stop thinking, spoke to invoke silence, made love to rid himself of desire, spent money to have none. He put so much money into building a house that we were left without one.

We moved in with his friends, Jon and Elsa, and their bull terrier, Pig.

&

Our bedroom door locked from the outside. Presumably, this was to keep Pig from bursting in and rummaging through clothes when we weren't home. She had in the past shoved stolen sandwiches beneath their piles; in our mess, they stayed lost until they began to smell. I didn't clean but continued to hope that past a certain point of disarray, things would begin to order themselves. Of course, this wasn't so.

Sometimes Crash locked the bedroom door and forgot I was still inside when he left. Maybe he never really saw me. When I ran out of cigarettes, I risked a shattered ankle and shimmied down the drainpipe. A crowd stood by to watch my descent. I dropped flat feet to concrete at less than a story, and headed for the tube.

At the entrance to the tube, a toothless old woman blocked my path. "Excuse me," I'd said. Although I towered above her, I couldn't get by. "Please excuse me," I said louder. Because she was smaller still for being two steps down, I bowed to her and caught eyes of colorless shine crumpled within a wadded paper face. I wanted to unwrap her, see what was written. I wanted to ask why the underground was closed to me, but before I could she sprayed spittle, shrieked, *"Fire."* And though I smelled no smoke, this origami Cassandra insisted that it was burning, back and forth, across the track, ". . . approaching like a drunk, in ragged repetition. It will swallow you up if you go down," she warned. The glint of mean in her message amused me—she must have been a failed poet; I dug for fare change, but found none. Naught for her, nor I—no difference to split. A sneeze of years and we might have been the same. She was right, of course; I should have been barred from an underground that didn't take credit. Crash had put my name on his VISA as a way of keeping tabs. But I wanted to lose myself, and looked to a blend of people, blur of speed, time, and distance to carry me. London cabs have limits. Besides, they loathe going beneath the Thames. I took this as a personal affront, and tried my best to avoid them, so, stuck above ground for God knows how long, I started to walk.

Kierkegaard said that if you keep walking it'll save you. But he died of exhaustion. I walked as if this disdain of destination would allow me to continue. As if my actions, my exits, were prologue. *I walked . . . and walked.* When I looked up to find myself a mile from where I'd last been, it astonished me. I walked until I came to King's Road, where I leaned against a wall and watched leftover punks with Manchester accents play with their dogs. The music that came from their box was a howl for the work that eluded them. They snarled at me, smashed bottles and spit, but they knew I loved their dogs too much for them to kick me.

I thought of staying, shaving my head, piercing my nose and joining their tribe, until, like a failed vagabond, I wondered if there was someone home to pick me up, to save me from the streets, from that rush of world that could lend me just enough character to keep walking. There was a phone nearby. I could have called collect. But if Crash was home, the look on his face as he pulled curbside would have been too much for me to bear; more and more, he abhorred being out in the open.

I stopped by a Chelsea kiosk, pinched a *Smash Hits* with Crash on the cover, and flagged a taxi. (Even though they never like going below the Thames.) When I arrived home, Elsa, the Gallic mistress of our temporary manor, she of the liquid eyes and exemplary breasts (a portrait is hung on the wall as a reminder), was making tea in the kitchen. I laid *Smash Hits* on her counter like an ace report card. It started with a piece called "The Great Spiritual Debate" wherein stars were asked if there was life after death. George Michael had answered, "Are we talking about the death of Wham! here or just personal?"

Elsa read this, rolled the magazine, and hit me with it.

I snatched it back, spread Crash's centerfold and read aloud: *This jazzman joined a proper pop group and PRESTO! He was a megastar. . . .* "Cool," I said, then read further. *Girls flock to him. The one he's got now won't last the year.*

"It eez awful to read zuch things, awful to have for a man a poop star!" said Elsa.

"Pop," I said. Pop, the father. Pop, the weasel. An infantile pronunciation—three letters long, then darkness.

I'd shrugged and sipped the tea she offered. Pig shuffled in for a pat, passed gas, looked behind herself, then quickly shuffled out.

Elsa's husband Jon is a stock car driver. Her own love could, at any moment, become engulfed in a great roar of gasoline flame. A sharp screech of brakes, brilliant burst of color—then nothing. A twice-split fraction of wrong turn could devour a world. This knowledge grants them a happy life.

They'd wooed across the Channel, married in Calais. And on their first anniversary, the ferry sank and Crash and I moved in.

‹ɔ

This was how Crash prepared for concerts: He kneeled before our CD player (first on the block), one hand on the bottle, the other on replay, and tried to remember hits he'd just recently recorded. He crammed like a schoolboy to retrieve into his mind and fingertips what it was that others liked—what it was that made him famous. Then numbed himself to this knowledge with repeated slugs of scotch. If the phone rang, he let it.

I've learned to let the phone ring too.

On its stand at the hospital, there's a snapshot I cherish:

One day when I insisted on using the tube, Crash, incomprehensibly, walked me down. A father who recognized his son's idol shot us by the mouth of the tunnel. In the photograph we appear happy. We hold hands; his grip is unequivocal—it states the import of mine to his. He doesn't want me anywhere without him, let alone in motion on public transport.

When I peer into that Polaroid present I remember the urgency of his callused fingers stroking my palm, like illegible braille. Remember him leaving, remember him walking toward the light.

"Don't look back," I said.

On the days we'd walked the streets together, we paused only to kiss. My lips swelled, not from sickness then, but from his taste. The looks from others lifted us. No gravity. No shame. Their smiles storied our lives, said we'd live forever.

He'd have died for me. If he could.

Now, when I'm shot with adrenalin to revive my failing heart, its beat comes to me an empty reminder—a fraction of feeling whose wholeness has left. And each time the doctors lay me with that ghost lover, and my heart pounds uneasily from its forced, false entry, it's as if I'm roused by a perverted piece of what had been taken. Like ash from the fire of my life come to tease me toward waking death. There's a crude loss that comes from having felt too much.

There was a time when life was high.

"This is living," Crash said.

"Like flying," I'd said. I should have said, "Don't look down."

Rise and shine, P."

"Mmm . . ."

"You were having a bad dream—something about a crash."

". . . bound to happen to a jet-setter."

"Well miss fancy pants, you mussed yours. Musta been some crash."

"Mmm."

"Help me out now, pick yourself up. Aw shit look who's—"

The doctors stand back, stare. Dismiss Gil when I'm clean.

"Things changed in an instant," I say.

"Just like that!? You saw no signs, felt no symptoms until the past month?" asks a visiting doc, come to see for himself.

". . . *BANG*," I say, "just like that." I answer their questions, but they can't comprehend.

My vivisectionists don't see the mural before them; they place specimens under a limiting lens, and so see only cells. Maybe it's because they're mast cells that the doctors expect something more—a message from the signals they imply. Shaped like flags. I can think only to surrender.

They can't ambush me like the others. At dawn, I'm awake. When they come for me, I give my blood, take their breakfast (the only meal I can eat) and fall sated into a stoned and sunlit sleep.

They fire Gil when they catch us.
   "Why not the nurse? Her shit doesn't stink, I suppose."
   "She has tenure."
   But I know better.
   "She doesn't share," they account.
   "But it helps."
   "It's not proper procedure."
   "It's how I can eat, sleep," I plead, but they shake their heads, a hydra in refusal of life's varied punctuation that encompasses the urge to go further. I want to shove them. But it's useless. In ignoring the need for interpolated clauses, life's little pauses, the hippocritic doctors exhibit a profound psychedelic sophistry.

I see Gil just once before he goes. He's not a waking dream, but an unemployed man at high noon, no regulation pocket for his heart, just empties packing bottom.
   My cells have become ants to the fast-disappearing lunch meat of myself. *Things change, in an instant.* I can sit up now due to the wonders of nerve damage, an excess of steroids has rendered my rear incapable of feeling. When doctors approach, I often goad, "C'mon—stick a fork in my ass." I'm done. My gums bleed so bad that the constant

taste in my mouth keeps me in childhood where, before teeth had the chance to hang by threads on their own accord, they were roped and ripped, tied to slamming doors. Gravity pulled me there, too, down now to seventy, the weight of a ten year old; I was counting backward, waiting to be born.

Gil fluffs my pillows, slips Sophocles beneath them.

"You not doin' so good, P."

"Sorry," I say. "Sorry . . ."

"Stop," he says. "Sorry's a sorry-assed word. Besides, this the easiest damn job to get, don't nobody else want it. I'm just taking a little vacation, paid, too. I ain't got no one else, nope, sold my estate, yessir, so I got no more pool to clean, no tennis courts to maintain," he winks, says "I'm nowhere, P. I'm free."

"I want to go."

"You're already there."

"I want away. I want free. Can we go?"

"I got no money, honey."

"We'll take the subway."

"It's cold out."

"Cold in here too."

When he leaves there's nothing to keep me. Sometimes at night I clutch tight at the sheets and feel if I let go I'll float right out that door I can now, sitting up, see. But I'd rather take the subway. If I were well enough to rise I'd ride it; I could pull a scarf on and be one with the world. We'd be the same. I remember how the eroticism of the underground, the continuity of individuals, comforts—if only for a short trip. So if I leave my body for good will this solace be sustained? I don't know. I don't want to die.

But doctors kill harder than paisley. I see my future dissolve before me, to a medicinal solvent haze. Still, I dream of amaranths. Crawl through them in my mind's eye— young, so young now. When the nurse comes to change me I snatch a needle from her baggy pocket, slip it, capped like a rocket, beneath my pillow. When she leaves I search and strike.

The night is illuminated by myriad white flags. POW. The momentum of exploding cells lifts me. I hover before a needle's-eye exit until I plunge through, start back onto the path, the infinitely long queue, the recursive, repetitive spiral that surrounds the finiteness of a life—the line whose design, apparent from above, is paisley.

I shut the door behind me and take flight past the hairless ghosts that line the institution. Awaiting proper procedure.

Fuck! Get some paddles in here—stat!" Domo says to the nurse.

"Stat this," she says. *I wonder what motion she makes. Hope it's lewd.*

"Get a grip," says the intern. *But she can't. Not without her fix.*

"Now!" says Domo.

"Better veg than dead, huh guys?"

"I told you she wasn't a good specimen," the visiting doc says. Domo throws a boxer's punch to my sternum—but he's a doctor, not a boxer. I feel a rib crack.

"How could her cells degranulate—we loaded her with so many enzyme blockers that I figured her kidneys would fail. So I found the brother . . ."

"He found you," says the visiting doctor. *Shit.*

"Damn," says Domo, "I just didn't expect more shock." The visiting doc checks me, his touch travels light, like he wants to leave such sickness, but not yet for good.

"Aw man—she's a mess. But alive."

I hear the nurse stomp. "Dr. Frankenstein, I presume," she says to Domo. And smacks down the paddles.

37

They have trouble finding a vein. Guess I'd used the last. Once veins were all they wanted. And I was proud of them, erect through my economy of flesh. That was before the bloat set in, the flesh flushed out. Before the veins receded, dry from suck, collapsed as if from the greed of unsatisfied children. When I'd wanted to leave, I could find no exit. I cradled my own arms, those gangrenous twins, and searched for a way out. I finally found a slip of blue beside a hematoma where green had joined pomegranate, so I plunged—and waited for the presence of all color.

Now all I see is red. The fluorescents flicker beyond closed lids. Then my hands are pierced. "Ow." A reflex, like Gesundheit. I say it, and squint against the light.

I barely noticed the hypodermic's prick with my usual low pulse, but its current gallop has changed things. IVs never hurt before. And they've always been in my arm. Now they're in my hands, stretching out atop my fingertips like rays—and suddenly I sense direction. Maybe it's manifested itself before me. Or maybe it's just my misbelief. I don't know.

"I don't know what happened," Domo says, then turns to the students. "Do any of you?" It's always the boys who are called on first. I think about answering the question. But I can't raise my hand.

They stop medication—they assume it didn't work, that it might have even caused my reaction. I'm too ill for medicine anyway. In its absence I rally. Days go by, then weeks. I can tell by the length of my fingernails (no one comes to cut them, and I can't use my scissors).

I try to eat. I'm hungry, but I taste nothing, so it's hard to continue. Harder still when Domo shows. "How's it going?" he says.

"Better," I say.

"We still don't know what made you worse."

"I do," I say.

"You do, huh," he says. He humors me with "huh." I ignore wordless wit.

"Want to know?" I ask.

"Sure."

"What's it worth?"

"What do you mean?"

"I mean you'll take a loss on that report of yours. What was it called? 'Stop Shock for Sure in Three Easy Steps'? Bet the bigwig pharm people in Michigan will pay a lot for it." ("Scary ph(f)arm people" Gil and I called them—we both feared such homonyms.)

"You're not one of those patients that wants to be a doctor?" says Domo.

"Afraid not. I can't cut what's human. So, if I tell, will you rehire the orderly you fired?"

"Can't. He didn't follow procedure."

"Okay," I say, and start to doze.

"He broke the rules," says Domo, loudly.

"Hmm—and the nurse?"

"You really want her fired, don't you?"

"No. I want him hired."

"So, what's your secret?" he says. I remain silent. "We found your brother, you know?"

"He found you. About time, too—he's a goddamn med student who lives a block away. You know?"

"Pre-med," he says, "and allergic to hospitals. We almost had to check him in the bed beside you—when he saw you he got all cold and clammy, said he couldn't take it, then mumbled something about an allergy."

"Aw jeez."

"Allergic to hospitals."

"Yes, well, aren't we all—give him some Seldane. And send in the nurse. When they show I'll tell."

My brother's eyes are bloodshot and he's trembling. We stare at each other in silence, until I say in a southern accent, "I wonder who Belle's fucking tonight?"

My brother smiles and embraces me awkwardly. Belle is the name of an Alabama cousin who came one summer to live with us. Soon after her arrival, my brother and I'd realized that Belle was a sexual predator who lacked the decorum to spare the few friends we had in common. This smack of incest made us uneasy at first, but we got used to it. In fact, we began to miss her when she wasn't around to embarrass us. On those nights that she was gone, we'd turn to each other, often out of nowhere, and say, "I wonder who Belle's fuckin' tonight." It became a kind of mantra, solace in times of boredom or dejection.

"I wonder who Belles's fu—" He cracks at the crux.

"It'll be okay," I say.

The nurse strides in followed by Domo and the gang.

"So, what's the hypothesis, sister?" says a student.

"She ain't your sister," my brother says, and sniffles.

"Let's suppose Gil gets his job back," I say.

"Why?" says Domo.

"Well, my nails haven't been clipped, my sheets haven't been changed. . . ."

"Shoot," says Domo. I reach in the bedstand, cop the syringe.

"*Shit.*" My brother has always been scared of needles.

"Hers," I say, and point to the nurse. "Things got boring around here, so I thought I'd take a trip."

"*What the fuck?*" says Domo.

"Morphine."

"What?" says my brother, still looking at the needle.

"You know—like Liquid Sky." I think of flightless birds. Drifting, drowning. And all at once I'm sapped. "The party's over." My brother nods, tired too, and makes for the door. Domo stops him.

"What now?" he says.

One day last spring, after a long absence, I'd surfaced on the twenty-six-inch set my brother won in a raffle. He and his friends had gathered after exams to wreak further damage on their overtaxed brains. Squints, his druggie roommate, noticed me first. "Hey, cool," he'd said. My brother, halfway through a fifth of bourbon, was just about to change the channel. "Your *sister*," said Squints. "Your sister. Cool." My brother had been looking forward to *National Geographic*. "Oh. Cool," he said. Then he saw me. I wore mirrored sunglasses, spike heels, little else. I wobbled a bit. Crash stood beside me. He wore silk and had hair that glinted ginger. Behind him stood a crowd of graytweeded schoolgirls. They screamed and sighed while I was silent. The aggressively perky MTV reporter pushed past me to ask Crash how it felt to fill Wembly five nights. "Sod off," he'd said.

"Isn't that the guy in Cultural Exhaust?" said Squints.

"Wasn't your sister in my physics class?" said a friend. But my brother just stared. "Hey, doesn't that guy get to kiss Diana Rigg in that music video?"

"Guess he gets to kiss everyone," said Squints, and switched to *National Geo*. "Will she ever come home again?"

"Don't know," my brother said. He'd never seen me so far gone.

Word of my recent existence reached my brother much in the way he'd learned of my former, but this time the show was not broadcast. This time it was not an ocean that separated us, but the cold concrete of an institution. His institution. The doctors inside didn't know how long I or my paisley could last, so they shot me, naked. A student snatched the tape. And so a year after my sighting I appeared, on another screen, in another pot-filled room just as my brother walked in. "My sister," he said. He didn't say "cool."

∾

I'm awakened that night by a stink, though I don't recall being ill. I reach for the bedside beaker, pitch myself over—but before I reach bottom, I'm caught by two strong-smelling arms, and swoon. A poor actress, happy to still be on stage. "Gil!" I say. "What the heck are you doing here?"

"Well, P., things got pretty boring out on the Riviera—

the titties all started to look the same. So I thought I'd drop by for a visit. Make sure you were all right and all. I been hearing rumors," he says.

"Like what?" I say.

"Well, Domo says you're a hazard, that you disregard procedure; the boys say you scare them; and the nurse says you got it right—so P., how you been?"

"All is well," I say, "but I guess it's me those nervous Nellies'll kick out this time. They don't have much good, med-wise, to say about me either. I'll be gone soon, Gil."

"You been feeling worse?" he says.

"No, better. Mostly."

"What about right now?"

"Much better—and thirsty."

"Take this," he says, and lifts a cup, just like the ones in cheap motels, wrapped for highway men and fallen women.

"Thanks Gil," I say, and sip. "If I don't go, they'll kill me—though I don't know what for."

"For science—or maybe to free up a space," Gil says.

"Yeah. People are dying to get in," I say.

"You're crazy, P."

"Still? After all these smears?"

In my presence, the doctors search tomes—not for hematic insight, but to find what might make them liable. And when I live, they want me gone as soon as possible.

They avoid me, and, without their assault, I continue to get better. I gain weight, gain space on my skin. The bruises are first to go, then, like winter delayed, just a leaf or two of paisley.

～

I delight in this well spell; the composure of body and clarity of mind is, to me, better than all the fishes in heaven. I look forward to strolls around the ward, though I must control myself. This mixed sense of joy and confinement instills in me the urge to run (well, shuffle swiftly, maybe) down halls to knock nurses' caps off. And, now that I can make sense of immortal passage, I can't wait to read.

But the cart has gotten grimmer. I scan torn *Life*, and *TV Guide*, though I only watch on Sundays—*60 Minutes* for the fear of god, and *This Week with David Brinkley*. The maniacal laugh of a man with intractable tenure pleases me. But it's not Sunday—it's Saturday night. So I step out, travel light; I'm untethered (I can feed myself now), and, thanks to steroids, can barely feel the ground beneath my feet. I'm tired of the stale stares and hushed complaints of elderly inmates—I want to see babies scream. But there's no one around to direct me to delivery; most of the staff is away—the doctors at their castles, the nurses in their bathrooms. I move through empty halls, and try to divine birth. Even if I have to stand behind glass that reflects my own arid eyes, I need to see babies snug and sleeping—I want only to gape at this garden.

"Only parents are allowed past this point," says a striper, and picks up the phone to report my transgression. I walk away as quickly as I can, but because my feet seem foreign, the floor becomes me. The volunteer is peeved by my fall. "Please," she says, "just stay down. It's not my job to pick you up."

"Of course," I say. "Sorry." When she's out of view, I leave the innocents and make my way to children, whom I can see are already sickened and sullied by their short stay in this wicked world. The only adults around are a middle-aged couple with a child I haven't seen before—and probably won't again. She's seven, or so. She still shines, but she has the bloat. Enormous bears flank her like anchors. The other kids seem annoyed by the scene. The parents are divorced, you can tell by the size of the bears. "You'll be fine," says Dad, and tucks the girl in. Mom tries to coax a smile by pulling up a playmate and dancing. The veterans frown at these three old children and their immense fictions. Then Beller, the paraplegic athlete, sees me and shouts, "Hey, I thought you were dead." I wonder if his voice broke in the hospital, realize this is the first time I've heard it.

"Go fuck yourself," I say. The parents gasp, the children clap. "Where's Charlie?"

"Gone," says Beller.

"Oh," I say. Somehow I thought Charlie could endure indefinitely.

"What about Austin?" I say.

"Home." I realize he speaks now to break the silence.

"A new home?" I ask, hopefully.

"His mom, sister, whatever, came to get him—she was bruised up worse than you—so I guess it's the same old," he says. *Not for long.* I pick up the primary-colored xylophone sticks and play a few strains of "Frère Jacques." I wonder if Charlie has new sticks, if they're wild with a blue from beyond, a blue to finally soothe. He is sleeping. I wonder what the tune played upon Austin's head will sound like with such color, I wonder how soon we'll hear it. "So, where you been?" Beller says.

"None of your goddamn business," I say, scan for oxygen, then light a cigarette stolen from my nurse. The parents leave in a huff. We laugh, I pass it on, and the athlete takes a toke.

"Are you a virgin?" he says, when the youngsters start to doze.

"Me? No. But I feel like one now, you know?"

"Yeah . . ." He stares down at his pajama top, as if he's looking far inside the self he's stuck with, the one that he won't lose—if only for a frenzied moment—until he too is gone. "I feel like one too," says Beller.

That night I think about ruins and archaic explanations. I think about how *virgin* used to simply mean *unattached*. Temple whores were called virgin. I think about sex, and though I know it's as unlikely to me now as signals from Jupiter—I dream of contact.

More and more, Crash left me alone. Too young yet to love solitude; the span of time with him on tour began to take its toll. I gathered postcards, gleaned regret. When I phoned, a backup said, in the voice that launched a thousand hits, "He'll get back to you." Finally, he did. "You could have a child, my child."

"Later," I said. And begged for a friend.

"I don't want to be surrounded by silly little American girls," he said.

"But I am one."

Willa had just ditched her quarterback. She wrote ten-page letters describing how all her time with him was spent on the defensive, when finals rolled around she'd been too sapped to study. Still, she aced the "Psychology of Sex Roles" test. Willa's loose-leaf reeked with the musty stacks and pencil shavings of my forfeit. I needed her, for redemption. When spring break came I sent a flight voucher in a card with a faux-Lichtenstein woman whose balloon read, "If we can send a man to the moon—why not all of them?"

❧

Willa's plane circled London in fog for hours. When it finally landed, the driver whisked her starved and spent to the BBC, where a woman with a purple crew cut crowned by a headset asked her if she'd like to dance onstage during the taping. "You'll add to the atmosphere," she'd said, looking like a large poisonous insect. She spoke the words like they were hers, but we could hear the original request by wire.

Willa bore teeth like angry peppermint. "I don't feel like whoring for you," she snapped.

Crash paced, pulled fags from a pocket of the lime kimono that made him look like a haggard horse-faced housewife. He heard Willa and stopped. "Sorry," he told her. "I promise we'll have a nice meal soon."

"I don't want a nice meal soon—I want food *now*."

Crash slid green and spindly from the stage, and brought a bowl to Willa. He's unsure how to calm my ever-crankier playmate. "Crisps?" he said.

Willa refused. "Chips," she said, "are bad for my complexion."

"Bloody hell," he slurred. "Sorry. Sorry. I'm sorry luv." Willa and Crash were homonymically pissed. He'd prepared for the gig as usual: seated before the CD player, beside himself, besotted.

"You look hot luv." Crash took my hand. I wondered what he meant. I was feverish. He left to get dressed, and I turned to Willa.

"Chips," I conspired. She grabbed some from the bowl, and the lead singer from the opening act sauntered over to share.

"I'm Terence," he said and postured. "Terence Trent D'Arby."

She giggled, we smiled. His mouth was hungry but mine curved as if keeping down a bad meal. "He's pretty," she said.

I shrugged. "C'mon then, let's watch his show."

Terence stood at the edge of the stage, bobbed his body three times like an exuberantly damaged child and bowed his head as if to pray. Instead, he abruptly flipped his braids. Then he stopped, shook his head, and yelled, "No. No. No, it was all wrong." Willa and I looked at each other expectantly. The crowd shifted uncomfortably with the disruption of their communal body sway; this *was* a live taping. Takes were supposed to be limited, and that was our ticket out. Before Willa starved. Before dawn. Crash hated to be awake at dawn.

Terence came out again. The same thing happened. When he came out a third time he stopped the number again, but this time he seemed a bit more satisfied.

"Almost," he said. It was then that we saw what he was after in this, his very first television appearance. His *braids*. The arc of his braids as they flipped from his prayer must be a perfect foil. A swelling manifestation of his magnificent mane. A wave upon which audience expectation could ride the crescendo of his cries.

"Oh . . . my . . . god," I said.

Willa's stomach growled.

This repetition went on until the director was forced to cry out "Beautiful, gorgeous, lovely locks" with each consecutive flip until Terence was finally placated, and his song, the show, began.

Terence's voice strained and screeched like James

Brown trying to signal distant planets. Aneurysm was in the air. But the song was catchy. Very catchy.

"Stay ay hay ay ay . . ." Terence screamed. "Let me stay."

After a short break, Cultural Exhaust performed their recent hit—Crash played like he was picking lint from the chords. Then, mercifully, we were off.

Willa sat in the front with the driver. "I get carsick," she said, rolled a joint on his dashboard and inhaled deeply.

"Can't she do a drug that doesn't smell?" Crash said. I winced. "Oh sweets, sweets. I'm sorry. It's just that . . . just that . . . I love you." A non sequitur to be sure. But he used the phrase like soft cotton wool. And I was wrapped.

"That stuff'll stunt your growth." His hand's on my breast.

"Cheeky," I said.

"Musta gone straight to your beard then," said Willa, alluding to the spotty growth on his face. Then she whisper-screamed in manic falsetto the song that had insinuated itself into the da da dum of our minds, its beat alone raison d'être. *"Stay ay hay ay."*

"Mmm. So what did you think of him?" Crash asked.

"Him? Puh-lease. Him and his bony ass?"

"The music, the *music*, Willa," he said.

"Hmm. Doggerel. Catchy."

"A bit over the top—don't you think?" he added. But Willa was already gone, listening to The Cure on her walkman.

Crash heard their buzz. "Puh-lease," he said.

∽

The Cure were my favorite. Their riffs sounded like an amplification of Urdu. "Paki noise," he called it. The Cure, too, ailed Crash—he said it had to do with their hair and makeup, their habit of cutting albums in France. I couldn't help but think that there should have been something more to his aversion, something bigger than geography and eyeliner.

It was dark now, quiet out. London closed early. Too still for a Saturday night. Date night. I sang the discordant song that the Persian League of Anti-Defamation was up in arms over. But they just didn't get it. It was my favorite, the one about *L'Etranger*.

Willa didn't last long in London. She started out on the couch, but was moved after confrontations with Crash. She saw him skulk past her one morning on his way to the loo. He wore only his red and black, hammer and sickle boxer shorts, so she'd shouted, "Aha! I always knew you were a communist." He almost jumped from the skin that so mortified him. Then he fled the room.

"Why is he so upset? Pop stars can't get blacklisted. Can they?" Willa asked.

"You embarrassed him."

She was stupefied.

"You made fun of him undressed," I said.

"That's ridiculous. He had shorts on."

"Underwear," I corrected.

"Oh good lord, they're no different than bathing trunks."

"Yes, well, he doesn't wear bathing trunks. He even dresses for the beach, not that anyone can catch a burn in Brighton. He's been like this since he was twelve. That's when he decided he wanted to become a monk."

"You've got to be kidding. Hey . . . wait! The queen. The queen's hotel was bombed the day after you sent me that postcard from Brighton—*C-Communists*," she stammered, in a shock of recognition.

"It was IRA," I said.

"Sure, that's what the government wants the Brits to think."

"Willa, Crash *loves* the Queen."

"Yes, of course—that's what he *wants us* to think."

The next day Crash packed for Holland. He'd been asked to special guest on a show. "Amsterdam sure sounds fun," said Willa. "Wonder if those brownies are as good as they say?"

"Try this instead." Crash threw her a sock, slammed his suitcase, and left. He hadn't offered to take us, didn't call until just before the live taping. "You can watch, if you want," he said. He played solo, acoustic. His voice, stripped of pretense, was shocking with need.

"Wow, he's good huh," said Willa.

"Yeah. Huh."

"Crash was bomb—ay?" Jon and Elsa called with congratulations from France where they spent summers. But Crash didn't come back that night, or the next. I waited by our window, a terrified curtain. Alone, I couldn't sleep. I wrapped myself in his robe—but he didn't have much of a smell. I shivered from uncertainty and walked the halls. Pig yawned behind me. If I tripped over the span of material, she barked in offense. In the morning, I was too sick for breakfast, too weak to make tea. Willa went to the pub without me. Brought back bangers and mash. I retched. Then I started to cry.

At nightfall I still hadn't stopped. *". . . Friends for life,"* Willa said, and moved into my room. "It's so damp here. How can you stand it?"

"I like the rain."

"Since when?"

"It's good for the skin."

"Yeah—well, yours looks like shit."

"Yeah." With her warm form I was able to sleep. She snored, but I was grateful.

I didn't hear Crash come in the next morning. Just saw him loom above us. Silent. Stricken. "See, told you he'd be back soon!" said Willa.

"You're in my bed."

"Helluva lot better than the couch."

"It's *my* bed."

"Geez, Crash. Bet 'plays well with others' wasn't your strong suit in school."

"Out!" Willa hops up. She's wearing his sickle shorts.

"I'll take them off." She made a motion.

"Don't." He pointed to the door, closed it behind her. "I need *privacy*." What he meant was: *You're mine.* "I'll run you a bath," he said. "And get *her* a bed."

Crash held the receiver in one hand, a Dunhill in the other; the mattress company had put him on hold, to see if they could deliver that afternoon. Between drags he continued with his mantra, "Privacy . . . privacy . . ." I placed my saucer beneath his precarious ash. "Can't I get *any* privacy?" he said.

"That's kinda antithetical to communism, don't you think?"

"Cheeky," he said. But he didn't smile.

～

Pig was overjoyed by the mattress—now she could sleep with the guest. Willa let her, notwithstanding her flatulence.

The morning Willa left to return to the States, Pig sidled up to her at the door, and sat beside her luggage, but when Willa tried to say goodbye Pig simply thrust her head up and away, her magnificent jaw stalwart beneath tiny eyes, disconsolate with perceived deception, that fixed on some far point until Willa was gone. When the driver slammed the trunk, Pig trumpeted a gaseous Taps for the loss of her bedmate, then bowed her head at such looseness (both of feelings and of bowels—she was an English dog), clacked a dirge with nails that Willa had freshly clipped (Pig allowed no one else) until she reached the loo, and hurled her heavy form over a wall of porcelain to seek refuge within an empty tub.

If you're well enough to run rampant around the ward, you're well enough to go home," says Domo. He looks angry, but I can tell I've earned his admiration. I won't just lie still like the others. Take everything from the white-coats, even a con, because I think that life is mine to keep (if everyone was as rich as Walt Disney, there'd be freezers from here to eternity). I've refused further treatment. Domo won't applaud my decision, but he admits it's a choice. Finally a choice. I feel power as I flip through the release papers—a thousand watts of will. Perhaps I'll harness it to survive—or if I've cut the line by leaving—go out in a brilliant firecracker burst—even if there's no one around to say "Aah."

When my brother arrives, I tell him I won't stay long.

"Why not?" he says.

"You need your couch."

"That's silly." He offers a sugar cookie. He's been eating the box he brought me; granules cover my sheets like someone else's day at the beach. "Seldane makes me hungry," he says.

"Well, sign this and let's get lunch." I hand the release papers to my brother.

"Today?" He chokes.

"Be at the main entrance by noon," I say, and summon Gil.

"Your chariot awaits." Gil puts me in the chair, whistles "The way you look, to-night," and wheels me past hangers-on. When I see my brother by his car, I tremble. I suddenly feel as if I've been a child lost for years at some Sears and Roebuck, now finally face-to-face with the family that's come to bring me home. I don't want Gil to witness such mush. I haven't missed anyone, and, soon, I'll leave the home I never had for a country where no one can follow. Still, I can't stop the tremble.

"Do you have a cigarette?" I ask my brother in the car.

"No, and you can't smoke in here," he says.

"Why not?"

"Brand new. Can't you smell it?"

I do, and it makes me vaguely queasy, just like the road he's on. A straight shot to suburbia. He wants me on it with him; he wants our kids to play together. I wonder if the mother of his will be more than a dim consideration. I want my brother to consider more. Consider this—that my blood, so like his own, multiplies, but resists replication.

"Why even have a car in the city?" I say.

"So I can escape."

"Have you?"

Crash's sister never left the Isle of Wight. To visit her, we ferried across the Solent strait. Before we arrived at her home (his old) we'd stopped by a chapel surrounded by statues. "I should have been a monk," Crash said, and showed me the stones he'd aspired after: a multitude of glaring marble martyrs. The caustic curdling upon their own bodies was no cause for concern for they were all eyes, all accusal. Their faces shone in effortless superiority to what was happening *down there*.

"Look. Look at them," Crash demanded.

"St. Genevieve?"

"She stood her ground."

"Yes," I said.

In any war there are skirmishes, small victories that ruin one with hope.

The next morning he snuck up on me in the bathtub, held me there and yelled downstairs for his sister to go on to church without us—that we'd overslept, would make her late. Then he got in behind me, enshrined me in his arms and, with the intention of a baptist, he washed me.

Crash, himself, seemed to be made of water—Neptune's child. Touch, the truth he fought against, lingered, demanding itself to be known as the one reprieve we are granted from our terrestrial trickery. Furtive need dissolved into a sea of hours, in which we lay, extravagant and idle.

It was in this peace that the paisley appeared. Violent blossoms upon my stomach and calves. My first instinct was to contain them. They continued to spread. *"God,"* I said.

"Whassit?"

"Look." I lifted a leg.

"Wash it off," he said. I couldn't. He didn't try to. Just backed against the tub. And stared, as if I was wrapped in spurge. Pretty poison. "Was the water too hot?"

"No," I said, "it was perfect."

"It's cold now." He got up, got out. Emerged stainless. "You'll catch your death," he said, and handed me a towel. Then he cleaned the tub, as always, to bid the swill of sentiment farewell, clockwise away. Also, to check that he was on earth, in England.

When we'd last strolled his island, studying scattered gouges, examining relics of battle, he said to me in resentment, "America has no scars, no marks from the war."

Back then I wore Pucci—on the outside. Beneath it my skin was faultless.

My brother begs me to cover myself. "Can't you get some pants on?" he says. I lie on his couch, stitched and broke. I bleed, I read, I try not to come undone. I try. My underwear is riddled with holes. I'd called such slack cotton "period panties," but the blood that spots them now is a clean clear red. My cycle stopped eons ago; I've since been hurtling through time untethered.

"I consigned my pants to a shop," I say.

"Oh," my brother says. He doesn't ask why. He knows the hospital took my last cent, that I was left with what was left of Crash's credit card. Knows I've consigned myself, too, to his couch.

"Hated those limey duds," I say unconvincingly. "Except for maybe those rubber Westwoods, or that pair of Katherine Hammets."

"You can wear mine," my brother says.

"*You* have Hammets?"

"What?"

"Nevermind. Just drape a sheet over me."

"It's less for my benefit than for Squints's."

"For appearance's sake," I say.

"Whatever."

It's my brother, specifically, whom I make uneasy. Baring my blistered buttocks in broad daylight is, to him, a reckless act. But the biopsies abide, and I care nothing for clothes. Besides, Squints doesn't see me. Squints perches on the fire escape, and fixes on the farthest point. He just got back from scoring some dope. If he did see me, if he hadn't copped, it wouldn't matter. He'd fluff my pillow and remain unmoved.

Squints wanders absently through the room, my brother offers me an afghan. I refuse its acrylic scratch. The slight breeze from the open window feels good on my stitches, but anything harsher, the brush of a blanket or pull of elastic, is painful.

"Can't you *please* get some pants on?"

This time the slap of my brother's disapproval is poked through with needles. My eyes leak useless tears. "It's just that . . ." He's doing his best to soothe me.

"Sorry," I say.

"Squints has been using my checkbook again to order pizzas," he says. I can see he's trying to draw me into his reality by using its focal point—cash. "Why didn't you go through with the procedure?" he says. He presses for procedures. I question that any sequence of steps can determine a life. I wonder for a moment which procedure he refers to, then I reach for the half-empty bottle before me. My brother snatches it away. Alcohol is forbidden. "It degranulates mast cells," he says in his doctor voice.

"Fuck it," I say. My cells are already crushed out of control, into a billion generative parts that blast forth pigments and poisons. Alcohol's properties (unlike anaesthetic) are too dilute for finality—plus I'm so insubstantial that, sometimes, if conditions are right, just an ounce can quell my senses, make me small enough for exhaustion to shove through the fast-closing window to unconsciousness. It's a precarious escape. Sometimes Pain races back, he beats me. Leaves the bed a prison, my pillow hot. Sometimes he forces me upright, and wills me to dance against the boozy backdrop. Pain is an abusive spouse. He always returns to find me sneaking off. And if he catches me—after much shaking and slapping—my faithful groom embraces me, and swears he'll never leave.

"Please give the rum back," I say.
 "So much sugar, doesn't it make you sick?"
 "I am sick."
 "Wouldn't you rather have scotch?"
 "Sure, why not," I say. "Let's have a scotch."
 "You've had too much already."
 "Get the scotch," I say. He does. We sit. We drink. In silence. Until he sighs and I sneak away.

My brother drinks, but won't do drugs. Squints doesn't mind; he prefers the nebulous existence of a solitary drug-user. He's never used drugs to open others (as is the fashion of men), and chooses to remain unescorted. I suspect Squints sees me as part of his hallucination, and take such familial consideration as compliment. Perhaps when he's lucid I exist as a flashback. Either way, my appearance never disturbs him. For this I'm glad, but the possibility of his genetic alteration concerns me. A doctor who works at the University had asked him for a sample of his spinal fluid. Squints balked, but when the doctor offered him five hundred dollars, he bit his lip and conceded. After he paid my brother for back-pizzas owed, he bought mescaline and spent the rest of that week communing with the STOP sign at the end of the block.

"STOP," he repeated. And after silences upward of hours, past rotations—the moon rising, the sun setting— he intoned again.

"STOP."

One night my brother and I brought him a Coca-Cola and a Milky Way, junk(ie) food, along with the imposition of a turkey sandwich. But he was gone from his corner. We found him further down the block, eyes wide in alarm, kneeling silent before the DEAD END sign.

◆

Autumn has come. I huddle into myself, hating the smell. Squints stays out on the fire escape, feeding pigeons. He's unmoved by weather, but the chill is too much for me. "Squints, please shut the window," I say. He closes it and locks himself out. He's still among the birds, except for the motion of his lips. I wonder what he tells them, if he explains the trickery of seasons to them—that, little by little, days die in summer. And, in coldest winter, light grows.

Squints's rapping breaks my reverie, but I'm too weak to lift a window. I call my brother and he comes to criticize. "I *told you* not to feed the flying rats again."

"They're pigeons," says Squints. "Rats can't fly."

"Well, wash your hands. And where are *you* going?" my brother asks. I've pulled his jeans and sweater, both cuffed like handouts, over my long underwear (two pairs).

"The Dublin House," I say.

"Good God," he says.

I shrug. I can't help it, my mind is as unquiet as the flapping of wings at Squints's exit. I need to walk the block—like a vampire without its bat, to a bar dark enough to hide in, with riff-raff rough enough to take me. I'm the belle of the ball in long sleeves and a turtleneck—at least for a few hours before fatigue squashes me. I usually spend time with a Vietnam vet who went in at sixteen a patriot and came out at twenty a wreck. But we can't get past our commonality, and the promise for further contact flags.

The next time I go out, again under the cover of night, I visit a boy who, years ago, had been consumed with me. I ask him to keep the lights out, but he sees the marks. His eyes bulge at the stigmas, visible in moonlight, before him. I'd shown him the ruin of his youth. He continues to stare, paralyzed by the shame of it—I am a Goya left out in the rain. His gawk goads me, and I run home for the last time, repulsed by his pity.

∽

Before I leave for good I take my brother's car, and drive south to see my parents. " 'Rents," my brother calls them. I like this term; it seems to break their hold—ensures that their possession is temporary. I use a rural route, U.S. 13, thinking the landscape will soothe me. The flattened expanse of nowhere is neutral, empty of any promise, save a butterscotch milkshake from the only landmark, a Dairy Queen up ahead. But I don't stop. I've lost the taste for sweetness. I ride tobacco roads through peanut towns, and light a cigarette, American; it tastes like glass. There's a sign now before me: ISLE OF WIGHT COUNTY—14 MILES. I think of the first, and as I near its reflection, I'm reminded that solace lies not in land but in distance. The current remoteness of loved ones calms me. Fear of death smells like burnt feathers. I turn from it to face away, into the moment's breeze, flush with motion.

I was always leaving, always forbidden to go. I started leaving at age six. My mother was supposed to pick me up from day camp and take me for a swim. She couldn't swim, but I wasn't allowed to go without her, so I waited in the heat until my suit got sticky, until the children and teachers left, until I was alone—then I waited some more. When I'd had enough of waiting, when waiting began to scare me—that's when I left, that's when I began to walk.

I walked and walked (with such short legs, I required then, as now, more steps to get anywhere). I walked miles to get back home, but the door there was locked. So I lugged a lawn chair beneath the shade of a chestnut tree, and sat. (The neighbors later said I'd looked cute, but they never thought to offer me in.) This waiting expired quicker than the last, and I walked back, unafraid, to where I'd begun. In the meantime, my mother was drawn to water. She careened around the pool, and demanded its lifeguards search bottom for the body.

In my teens, my mother still searched. "Where are you?" she said.

"Outside."

She peered from the kitchen window. Her hush was a holler.

"You look disgusting. That swimsuit's up your crack. How can you move like that?"

"I'm not moving—I'm reading." The sun, the shine on my skin, the words of a far civilization, made me happy.

When I was little, I'd snuck like a lover to see the world. I spent milk money on candy, just to hear the lilt of the shopkeeper's distant tongue, see his old-man's eyes like a river at dawn reflect a me I didn't know. I risked being found out. Risked being knocked down by a nearby dog who played rough. I gave the candy to my brother. I didn't much like sweets—did like the world.

I was knocked down, found out. I lost four teeth. My father put them in a glass of pop as punishment. Beneath a pillow, they'd have been worth a dollar. Each night, I was pulled from my books to watch rot. My brother said nothing—but later offered me his allowance. I refused; it was dirty money.

I soon switched from sweets to smokes. The shopkeeper's were French, filterless; they smelled vaguely fecal. "I'll have a pack of those." I was ten.

"Smoking stunts growth," the shopkeeper said. "You'll stay small—then you'll die."

"Like you?" I said. He grinned, toothless too.

"I'm not dead yet."

"See?" I said.

"No," he said, and sent me off with a pop.

I weighed the risk and walked to the grocer. When he too said no, I sent the bum outside in with enough money for a pack and two beers—one for us each. The bum's name was Waldo, at least that's what he claimed. He said he had trouble finding himself. "I hope my own daughter doesn't smoke," he said. The next week I bought him a sandwich with my cigarette money. "I'm cutting back," I explained.

He took a small bite, then looked at the bread as if it were alive. "Thank you," he said. His sob surprised us both—just a little though, like a hiccup. I'd never seen a man cry, so I thought about this small sound and how it could signify, more than any bawl, bolt, or bomb, the enormity of absence that surrounded us. The force of his grown-up sorrow pushed back the sky that day, and I was certain I'd lost more than the inch I'd recently gained (notwithstanding the shopkeeper's decree).

When my family moved South, where children are encouraged to smoke, I met Jenny, a girl so infused with joy that she never stopped smiling—not an idiot's grin, but a pure one that I was convinced came from seeing only good in the world. Jenny had had an operation on one eye—it remained pretty useless, a permanent wink that went well with the grin. She was poor but her clothes fit (mine were perpetually big—I never grew as Mother hoped). I liked Jenny's clothes; they were patched with flowers and peace signs. Her parents were young, their hair long and lank as her own. My mother called them hippies, and said Jenny looked like Amy Carter. My father called them communists. I never could tell if he was joking. I liked Jenny's parents. When she turned ten like me they had a big slumber party for her. It was the event of the season. I walked back from school staring at my invite. I tripped once and was almost hit by our neighbor's car. When I arrived home I held it out, like a winning ticket. My mother said, "No."

"Why not?" I said.

"Location, location."

"But they're so close."

"It's a bad subdivision."

"If I get all As?" I bargained with good behavior. I weeded, I dusted. I begged to go.

"Communists," my father said, as if it was a punch line.

They finally gave in. But at nightfall, when the fun began, the party ended. My parents didn't permit sleep-overs.

Jenny's parents tried to help. They told me to phone home—as if my asking to stay could make it so. "The commun—The *compass*ionate people want to speak to you," I said. Jenny's mother glowed. Mine said, "No."

My parents rarely went anywhere together, so I was shocked when they both showed. Then I realized, by the way my father kept watch on his finned blue Plymouth, that he'd come for safety's sake. He stayed silent—he's always silent around those he thinks of as lesser—while my mother strained at small talk. "This energy crisis sure is something—I guess by the looks of it you all are splurging," she said. She pointed to party lights, but I knew her statement was spurred by Jenny's resemblance to Amy Carter—and this embarrassed me further. "Most people don't sit around with all the lights off, even in an energy crisis," I said. Jenny's parents just smiled, and sent me away with sweets. The children pitied me. I left with streamers stuck like rest room refuse to my pf flyers. Stayed up all night counting stars whose names I'd yet to learn, or had already forgotten.

My parents' recompense: I'm allowed to sleep, once, at a girl's whose mother came from the same neighborhood as mine. The girl and I try to build a tree fort, but when I don't please her, she takes to hitting me in the knees with a hammer.

⟊

I have trouble maneuvering my brother's car, and think for a moment I should go back. I've lost my nerves—in more than a manner of speech. An excess of steroids will do this. Certain parts of me have lost the ability to feel. My insensate foot rests too heavily on the gas. I surrender, and speed. Protest my time denied. I try to fix on the road before me, but my mind wanders ahead to my parents, the problems they present. And I careen into a blue Plymouth. No fins.

A man gets out. Gray sweats, gray hair. Gray day. Anger precedes him like thunder. "What the hell?!" he yells, and strikes his fist on my window.

"Things in my life are not very good." I open my door and look in the rearview. Atop my red blue riot of flesh there's blood: a tear shaped like paisley, in backward benediction from my bow to the dashboard. I let it slide, and try to think of my lips, full of cells' fall, as sensuous. Of imaginary collagen bills saved. Then scarlet streams sudden from beneath my skirt. The impact has opened a wound.

"Aw man." He misconstrues me. I go from ill to battered with a botched abortion to boot. I've become his guilt rolled into a road hazard.

"Must we wait for police?"

"I'm a cop," he says, over his shoulder. "Just . . . go."

I wipe myself, put on a fresh skirt, leave the old like roadkill. And tumble home.

My parents don't know how sick I am. My mother thinks I have allergies. My brother tells them I have asthma. What will I say? How will I sneak cigarettes? I'll need their soft sham of soot to survive my stay.

My God," Mother says.

She's come upon the paisley.

I should have covered my tracks, worn more clothes. She lifts my skirt like a cerement. At first all she sees is a darkened skin—then she bends closer and finds me covered, like a toddler at teatime, with grape jelly splotches. "Stay here," she says, as if I might not. She returns with her spectacles, and again, lifts my skirt. This time the scrolls come into focus, and she reaches for whitewash. "Plastic surgery," she says. "We'll just have to remove these."

"No," I say.

"Why not?"

"Because I'm barely dimensional—without them there's nothing left."

"Don't be absurd."

"It's true," I say, "look closer." She draws back.

"Well then, that's what you get," she says.

"What. What do I get?" She purses her lips. I know what concerns her more is what I won't get.

"It's just that . . . people will . . ."

"Fuck 'em if they don't like it," I say. But that's just the point—there won't be much fucking of them. "Them" will with time narrow out to nothing, "them" will stretch to an undiscovered string; they'll stick their fists through me and never know it.

Mother, too, is disappearing. She seems smaller when, in lieu of solidarity, she reaches up to kiss me. Her loss of faith shows in the cracks shot through her smile. A vacuum of regret. I feel its pull brush past my cheek. Sacrifice for her children has not, it seems, yielded all that she'd expected. My "life in sin" has angered her god.

If you go around naked, He'll do something to make you put clothes on.

She'd tried to warn me.

I'm dying to tell her the truth, but she's on the phone with another plastic surgeon. She labors to make light with them—she's flirting I think. I'm jealous of these would-be suitors, and the doppelganger daughter of whom she speaks. "Oh she's fine—just having a bad bout of allergies," she says, "she probably contracted it from the English food." I hadn't heard that one before. Last week she'd asked how my "cold" was, and blamed it on my not taking any tweeds to England. "Wool clothing encourages proper decorum," she'd said, before I left the States to live in sin.

"He's a rock star," I said.

"It'll please his family."

"Pink Floyd pleases his family." But mine misunderstands.

"Stick to mauve," she says. "It's more your color."

&

I've always hated mauve.

Now it's become me—a violent mallow through to the marrow. I'd rather be blue—floating, silent and still. But indelible cells rake roses to my surface, like petals from a plundered nursery. The color of flesh seems as strange to me now as the plastic dolls that line our attic. I imagine their eyes, blank and unblinking, their paste pupils split.

              ୬

My mother is still on the phone. "Yes, oh yes—she slept with an animal."

"Mother," I cry, but she waves me away. She's never before brought up the subject of my lover.

"It would kill your father if he knew about 'your boy-friend,' " she always said. She rejects his name, as if it might be an invocation. But this is the first time I've heard him called an animal.

"So—no matter what their size, they're all full of dander?"

I realize now she's speaking to an allergist about the dangers of dog hair. My parents always feared pets, so before mine I made do with strays. I suffered bites and mites. I even got cat scratch fever. But I was never allergic.

My dog, full of fur, is named Douglas, for the dark lake in her eyes. Also, because its diminutive sounds like the only name she'll answer to—she's a sublime canine, and consents only to the most general of identities. Where is she? I wonder.

I open the door, and my shepherd shoots in. A high-pitched wail escapes her. I slap my thighs, but Doggy doesn't dare jump, so I kneel to stroke her snout; wince when I see its scar: an absent brand amidst black, no longer red or raw, but the pale pink dressing of a little girl resigned to maternal rule.

"Just don't have any children; don't do me any favors," Mother told me.

I'd left Doggy behind to be spared British quarantine. She's confined to the kitchen lest she spread hair on rugs Mother wanted replaced.

"Your father won't buy me new rugs," she said, when I asked from London how things were.

"Make him buy you new rugs, buy your own rugs," I said. As if these, we, were the same.

"He's still going on about April's ice storm. We got the insurance check for the roof but he'd already sealed it himself."

"Nothing new under the sun." I hadn't seen it in months.

"There's been a few accidents," Mother had said, on our last call. Father wired the smoke detector so safely that leaves burned four doors down set it off. Doggy, alarmed, did not bark. Instead, she hyperventilated by my mother's bedside. This wheeze, not the siren, woke her. "The dog's not supposed to leave the kitchen." The next night she did it again. *Hufh, hufh, hufh.*" Mother snuffed for effect.

I held my breath.

"Children had come over that afternoon, shaken her up." She meant they disrupted routine. That night at four A.M. Doggy again breathed by her bedside. When she turned the flashlight on—kept by the bed for "acts of

God" or to dial 911 without alerting intruders—she saw blood drip from her snout. "Blood everywhere." Mother got up to see "why, how, where." Father, down the hall, slept on. "Had the dog been cut?" But she could find no sharp object. "She went in your room. A perfect stool. It didn't ruin the rug. I picked it up easily off the rug. But all around it, there was blood. At the foot of your bed there was blood."

I saw in my mind's eye how, nose to the floor, my dog had rubbed all around her shame, afraid to touch, to dirty herself. Wanting so badly to hide it.

"The blood won't come out. It's god's way of saying—I told your father—that it's time for a new rug."

"Kitchen," Mother says, and points to it like a pistol. The dog tucks her tail and slinks back, then dances and skitters on the edge of worn linoleum. "Good girl," I say. It catches in my throat.

"Don't let her lick your face like that."

Mother is still speaking into the phone. In spite or because of all her far misses, her marks have always stunned me. I suppose it's my mistaken belief—that she must look in my direction to see—that makes me vulnerable.

"She's not dirty—and I'm *not* allergic to dogs. I'm..." I want to tell her.

"I'll hold," she says.

She looks up at me now, and I squint hard, as if this might adjust her own view. It won't. So, how can I tell her that it's my, our, blood—the fluid of existence—that I can no longer tolerate.

To paraphrase Goethe: Life is short, but this afternoon is endless.

My mother makes plans that I'll never keep, while I begin a thousand sentences about my sickness—and finish none. Her sorrow will be bitter, her blame my pain. For her there are no accidents. And wellness is my responsibility. I've lost it.

In childhood, I was told to never drink from another's glass. I hid maladies, ashamed of my own carelessness. I masked colds, then suffered bouts of pneumonia and pleurisy. My lungs became scarred. When they healed, I smoked. (I got smacked if caught at my cuticles.) My brother sucked his thumb, but I'd ignored mine for fear of buck teeth and instead bit my cheek.

My fingernails are impeccable, I do not chew inanimate parts of myself.

I've never smoked in front of my mother. I'd like to now. I'd like to tell her the truth. I do neither. Instead I head for booze.

The liquor is tucked away, beneath unwrapped gifts and unopened candy boxes, in the corner of our unused dining room, where we eat only on holidays—and most times not even then. The cabinet held dusty bottles of schnapps and scotches, bourbons and brandies. It remained full throughout our childhood, as if waiting for some great event to set loose the vapors. My brother and I snuck sips and replaced the ill-gotten swill with water. After grade school, we plundered ruthlessly and left the store in its present state—an unfit prison, with only the weak and unwanted left behind.

I search the cabinet for the single-malt scotch that my favorite uncle, John, used to give us on holidays—but I can't find it, so I settle for a crusty Galiano. It sickens me to swallow so much sugar. Sweeter than rum. We never had rum. I drink; it helps. I need a new point of view. I need to shake the feeling, here in this house, that comes with television. I rarely watch it, but inevitably, when I do, the episode on is the one I saw last (which was also my first time).

Our set, the same since I can remember, is off. When my father shows, he'll turn on the news, and the black-and-white will blare nonstop disaster to his deafened ears.

"Mother, why don't you get a color set?" I say. But she doesn't hear me. She stands before her open freezer, and pores over wax paper packages, each wrapped like wedding cake. I wonder how she knows what's what. And if she sees the picture before me—the wall of frostbitten bricks. The life on ice.

"Why not a color set?" I say, again.

"Go ask your father," she says. "It's five o'clock." Five is their universal constant. It's always been too soon for my last meal. I snuck cereal while they slept—if I ate at all. Dinner at any other time drains my father. Five may be the hour of cocktails, kickball, or after-school kisses for others—but for my parents, it's dinner. And it's rarely delayed. Father always wanted to weather such anarchy of the kitchen, but his panic broke through, like cats in paper boxes. And Mother exploded.

I go to fetch my father for five. I wobble like a toddler from my glass of Galiano, and, on my way out, wander the halls in search of change.

Our house is eerie, but essentially the same. The wallpaper droops a little, like an old woman's stocking. The gilt mirror, that has always looked to me like some monstrous brooch, has begun to oxidize; I see spots break through, and look away. It's then that I notice the photographs hung in framed isolation on the walls are reprints. My father must have filed the originals away for safekeeping. These are beginning to dissolve. Tiny bubbles dot the images—my dead grandmother looks ill, and my own picture has faded to a preternatural pale as if the white paper beneath is taking over, peeling through. This horrifies me, and I drop my empty glass. It shatters. My mother appears in pot holder mitts. "Sorry," I say.

"You shouldn't drink before dinner."

"Mother . . ." I look at the window, watch twilight dance erratic on its pane, and wonder how to tell her.

"Geez but you make me nervous. What? What is it?"

"Nevermind . . ." I say, as she leaves, "it's just that the pictures are fading."

The trees in our yard have all disappeared, and my father sits filing their stumps.

I look to the sun, but it sets in accusal, and the last red rays of day raise the heady scent of malithion. Doggy sneezes and runs to my father. He pats her head, then shoos her away. He's always been unnerved by her presence; to him, the brevity of a dog's life places it just a doorstep from death. He looks down, afraid to look behind, as if he'll find the years there gathered like a crowd of white coats come to take him away. But it's just me, his squashed seed of immortality, broken link left dangling by the dog of me gone gate-crashing.

"What happened to all the trees?" I say.

"I don't like mildew," he says, and straightens, as if addressing the gravity of the situation.

I smell something besides malithion—the scent of stooped Saturdays spent gagging over blackened grout—a gas from the past that I realize is bleach. I try not to breathe; this, and the fact that I've intruded upon my father's last-ditch effort fells me. Trees bring water, water brings rot; the rot is resistant, so my father does away with the trees.

"It's almost five o'clock," I say.

"I'll just be a moment," he says, and retreats to his stump. He looks like he's glad to see me. He reaches into his pocket, and hands me a file.

My father had always been a fix-it freak. He even championed the local sand-replenishment projects—although he hasn't been to the shore since Coney Island, and has never worn swim trunks. Wool pants rolled, tools slung low, my father was our Vishnu—not the disciple of Siva, the destroyer, I see now before me. His plan had always been to patch. Our garage is still stacked with salvage. Crystal radios, canned goods, cigar boxes—but no cigar. My father's new car, a maroon Ford Torino over fourteen years old, won't fit. It sits in weather while he keeps watch over the elements (my mother had eventually set fire to his first car). Globs of varying purples—the maroon hue is irretrievable in the annals of auto paint—are visible on any areas that might have shown signs of rusting.

We left Brooklyn in the Plymouth. My Uncle John was so offended by the picture of us packed and loaded into such battered blue that he offered to buy my father a new car. My father, of course, refused; John's was dirty money.

John was a professional gambler. He embraced risk and married a lounge singer. She was the love of his life—and another man's wife. John had almost gotten himself killed.

Instead, he got rich.

Years ago, in my uncle's New York restaurant (he had another in Vegas), I smoked cigarettes, sipped scotch, and waited for Steinbeck's widow. (She'd order his favorite dish, and eat at the bar.) I liked to watch her chat with the bartender; he made her happy. I suspected that few on the East Side did. It seemed strange that she lived there. She'd looked the part, but I wondered if she felt misplaced.

My uncle asked if I remembered leaving the city.

"The Plymouth," I'd said.

"The Grapes of Wrath," he said. "That's what it reminded me of. Don't know how a man could move his family in something like that. His family, for God's sake."

When my uncle died this year, I asked my brother how Dad took it. "Pretty well—he had smoke to blame. Cigarettes were the *definitive* cause," my brother had said, in his doctor's voice. Perhaps my father thought that in their absence lay immortality. How will he comprehend the anarchy of my own state—that cells from his own could turn so savage? My father thinks that a natural state without exterior introductions is inherently a stable system. *Simple systems behave in simple ways; complex behavior implies complex causes.* It was what he'd been taught. He was a dedicated pupil, trained in classical physics, who never knew the universe never was what it was.

I never knew, exactly, what it was that my father actually did. Only that he was a civilian engineer who worked for the government—invaluable and underpaid. When I pressed him for a job description, he answered only, "Classified."

"What's that—on your leg?" he says.

"Classified," I say, not in cruelty, but for want of a better term. What did I do to get so black and blue?

My father looks again at my leg, and, as if in response, it begins to bleed. His eyes are impenetrable. In their gray glaze, I see only my reflection. My father blinks fast now, telegraphic signals. Sequences, series, seemingly random. New codes, far from the monstrous prism of childhood I still cannot crack.

"Why?" he says.

"Why what?" I say. His eyes clear for one brilliant moment, then he turns away, and for the first time in his life, he cries. His sound—like trying to contain the wind—scares me. I need him to stop. "Dad, please. I'm . . . okay."

"Crown and glory," he says, and stifles a sob.

He'd liked my hair. He notices now that some is missing. What remains of his own hair has been abraded to near extinction—like a lawn rendered dust by an angry gardener. He's lost weight too. He was always thin, but this new jut of bones makes him look like an escapee from some terrible camp.

"Why are *you* so skinny?"

"Rats," he says.

"Get a cat," I say. I'll say anything to keep from crying.

"Science," he says. "Rats fed a low-calorie diet live longer. The ones kept near starvation fare even better." My heart falls, as if I could give birth to it, place it, in the stead of a grandchild, into his worn and hungry hands. "How was your flight?" he says. He speaks haltingly, as if in need of a jump start, then he interrupts himself, "A DC-10 went up in flames the other day."

"I drove here," I say. And sigh. I feel better now that the conversation has taken a familiar turn. I grew up with disaster chitchat. Planes fell daily, and the red end was always near. I watched for a cloud to mushroom outside my flowered draperies, and—in spite, or because, of the imminent apocalypse—I loved to fly.

My father drove vast distances to escape even the briefest flight, believing that, on the ground, he was in control of his journey. He was one of America's most dangerous drivers, for he never adhered to the speed limit, but kept way under it. For good measure. For this he was ticketed twice. When my brother and I were children, we counted the cars that passed by, and watched with wonder the bottleneck backup our Plymouth could incite. *When flow is smooth, small disturbances die out. But past the onset of turbulence, disturbances grow catastrophically.* Fluidics became my forte. But my science was not my father's.

I kiss my father on his sodden, shadowed cheeks—even fresh-shaven this darkness will remain; he believes electric razors less hazardous. He'd given me one, dainty and pastel, on my thirteenth birthday. So much noise for so little blood. I bought Bics with babysitting money and scarred my shins permanently. "We should wash up," he says, and rolls sleeves the gray-blue color of captivity. I rise from what's left of the grass, and brush it from my ill-fitting skirt. "Mother will be upset by those stains."

"Yes," I say, and walk the other direction to finally sneak a cigarette. "I'll just be a moment," I call out. I'd parked my brother's car down the street, not just to hide its dent, but so my father couldn't change its oil. *You can never be too careful.* I pass his Torino—a movable patchwork against time, monument to his imagined war—and remember how embarrassed my brother and I were when my father spent time in its trunk. Dirty, sweating, meager, my father fixed things. I never knew what it was he fixed in the trunk. I never really knew my father. This I know—

that in youth his war was real. He'd served in the army, thrived in the Arctic. Firmly rooted to tundra, he grabbed signals from the sky his brothers flew in, unfolding and refolding transmissions like so much origami. Alone, he was a master of communication, he spoke in tongues to save the world.

When he kneeled shirtless in that open trunk, with his rolled wool trousers out of view, he appeared naked. He looked like a saddhu. But he never roamed. He came home every evening by five. He parked t-square straight—a job that sometimes took over twenty minutes. Back and forth, back and forth, closer—still closer. Sprigs of grass strained from the concrete edge. The green barely grazed his white walls. He never reached the desired position. Mother came outside each night at the sound of the idling motor, and in exasperation, demanded that he stop.

I cut across what's left of the lawn, step over dwarfed fence posts embedded with tiny drainage screens—talismans against the mildew. I look behind, and the house stares back white, perpetually startled. It should have been left to settle, to wheeze comfortably. Instead it's been made to stand straight.

I can do nothing to change this. I reach the car only to find my pack empty and—like the profligate, I leave to get cigarettes—and never come back.

My family smears the eastern seaboard like the skid of squealed brakes. I'd escaped this casualty by going farther.

I never meant to reach the edge.

Now, I feel as if I've lost it. With my frequent flyer miles, I can only go so far—Canada, or the Caribbean.

I stop to think at the beach. Virginia's is overcast, like Brighton. Sometimes seashores seem similar, as if one follows you to another. The difference is just a lap of light, slight of wave. Virginia is England by increment. I have always been an inhabitant of coasts.

Perhaps I'll always be two places at once, littorally.

I trade my miles for a free ride, and live my last days on Crash's VISA. Four out of five doctors say I'll be gone before the bill comes due, so I stiff them. Take the chance (the cash) others (myself included) don't have. I'll leave the car at the airport, leave no forwarding address. Then blow what's borrowed like the last October dandelion in a barren field. And slip without stir into stygian warmth. I'll die stealing, because I have no desire to die in abject poverty. If that were the case, I'd have spent what remained on a flight to India, and thrown myself in the Ganges.

But I dislike bathing in sewage. Plus, I'm spiritually devoid. So I choose a rock in the ocean, beaten and bashed, yet strangely, inexplicably, spared by the hurricanes that devour other islands.

I've found the rock to hide beneath. In the straight world, Barbados will be my beard.

I'd been there before. Alone with Crash. The water was safe, the language, English. Without it, I'd die adrift like my immigrant grandmother, whose words, because they weren't her own, were always directed toward others. Like her actions, like her life. In the end, she scrambled for words of her own, then gnarled them like the back of the laborer's hand she no longer knew. I'd held this hand and tried to render a view past her claustrophobic close, tried to translate to touch the words of others—sounds that stampeded only to halt at the jolt of this perimeter, like a gathering of expressionless cows.

The daughter in the kitchen spoke, soap diva on the set screamed, and children chattered at her feet. Favorite sayings became foreign. Grandmother was too far inside for a second language. She needed her first. The snapshots in her mind were not enough to tie a life together. In the end, there was no one to discuss such a lack of order, not even herself. She mumbled at the jumble until, finally, stark sentences spoken as if with cottoned ears came last ditch.

"Just dig me a hole."

"Grandma!"

"The Grandma you knew? She's dead."

I don't want to die so far from myself.

I need English, my own Germanic tongue, rough as a cat's—that solitary creature. I have no child to touch, to translate, so away, alone, I'll cling to the tyrant I'd twisted.

❧

You travel wid udders?" says a Bajan stewardess, on the flight to Bridgetown.

"Sorry?"

She sees I'm not well. "You going alone?"

"Yes."

"How long a stay?"

"Don't know."

"De singular isle she may try en keep you."

"Singular island?"

"Sure," she says, as if reminding me.

I realize then I've yet to inform friends I'd long left behind of my imminent arrival.

"Why for you goin?"

"Um . . . I like beaches."

"Mm, well stay safe, de sea ain' got no back door."

I take heed, gulp the soda she offers, and burp contented. Accidentally. The child across the aisle smiles. Her father scowls and shields her from something stronger than bad manners. Maybe it's my skeletal frame that bothers him. Perhaps parts of peanuts are visible atop my swollen gums. Then I realize it's the paisley, and pull down my sleeves.

Many by now have died with marks. Felled by some aspect of blood, as of yet, unknown. It doesn't matter that though unwell, I am spared AIDS's acronical certitude, that my cells don't die but procreate in extreme. Now my catholic cells, unchecked, have the children I'd refused Crash, a teeming violence of missionaries—their apparition mirror image to the deadly acronym. The stares from men that once coveted my skin, now cut. Alien can be worse than dead. I look too dark to them now, as I had to Crash, like a Paki. He thought my blood was his punishment. That it seemed to have gone bad by itself implied to him divine wrath. I could not offer dice in its stead; I would never be able to impress the meaninglessness of my marks upon him. The same arrogance that brought him notoriety told him his god had time to play favorites.

A static snap crackles from the speaker like the briefest of bolts. *Prepare for landing,* says the voice I thought I'd hear more from along the trip. Then, as if in consolation, the stewardess gives me a tiny bottle of Mount Gay. The drink is mystic. Barbados is a rock, and a rock is not arable. Sugar is a rich man's crop, yet Bajans beget sugar from stone. Still, sugar doesn't sell. (Now the world uses corn syrup.) With so much sugar left unloaded, the land is rife with decay. Bajans hate to complain—the quarters are too close.

The Caribbean is soaked in bad blood, but a rock will not reabsorb it.

 ∾

In the airport, beneath Mount Gay murals, an elderly British couple confront their tour guide. They're as spherical as the young woman is sharp; she looks like she could burst them. "But the commercial . . ." they say, again and again. "In the commercial the islanders were white." *They must be kidding.* "This is *not* the holiday we planned." The hidebound Brits refuse to move. I drag my suitcase past them to immigration. It seems heavier now; I've packed too many jars of peanut butter, too many books. Underwear you can wash. I feel faint, achy, icky, in a way that seems to come, for a change, from outside myself. I feel like I drank a gallon of my father's wine, like I ate a pound of take-out Canton, wanton with msg. I'm drawn with a deep dehydration.

The three old men before me in line dab with white pressed handkerchiefs at tiny beads atop their brows. "Man oh man, we on CPT." I wonder how the idiom traveled and if it was the same as in the States, then realized, no, it must be *Caribbean* people's time they speak of—a different derision indeed; their mockery is good-natured, this proclamation their own. It seems they've returned victorious from a tournament. I look at their enormous trophies and they beam like boys. *What could these paunchy, peckish old men excel at? Bridge? Maybe there's a seniors league in cricket.* "Are those for cricket?" I ask.

"Girlchild you must be funnin'," the oldest says. Silver hair frames his ancient, unlined face like a spaceman's helmet. He looks like a time traveler untouched by hours. "At our age da only ting left ta do is gamble."

"An we da masters." The bald one pats his trophy. His head is shaved, so you can see how shadows are darkest at the hollows of a man, but fade near the edges, like silk left out in the sun. His skin, like the others, nears the spectral absence of the aged. Of my muted grandmother, of the dissatisfied couple immobile at the gate—of us all, should we be so lucky. Centenarians are all the same color. A gray gleam of light.

"Yeah mon." The youngest, seventyish and spry, lights Dunhills off his butt and distributes them. "At Domino, we da champ!"

Of course. I want to ask them how to play this game of irrevocable finality. But the immigration officer interrupts. "An where you goin girl?"

"There." I point outside, past glass doors. Beyond this border.

"*Your address.* What will it be for the next few months?"

"I don't have one."

"No?"

I sense my answer's not acceptable, so I change it. "I'm staying with a friend."

"Who's your friend?" he asks.

"Tomas . . ." I realize I'd lost his phone number, forgotten his last name. I can neither access the length of his hair, nor angle of his smile. The color of his eyes changes in my mind—blue to green to gold-flecked brown; the kaleidoscope of memory scrambles the print. Still, I strain to see, but sight slides from time like tears off a rheumy eye, and the thing that remains is his scent—a buttery must of salt sea and post-adolescent oil. *Almost like popcorn.* I don't think the officer will appreciate this, so I try to explain Tomas's neighborhood. "I'm not sure, um, what his address is exactly. He lives with a few other boys. . . ."

"*Other boys?* Boys here live with they family, not each other."

"They're medical students," I say.

"Oh. So he Trini?"

"No, no he's Portuguese."

"What? Why come so far?"

"He lives here."

"We Bajan here—he backra?"

I shrug.

"He a white boy?"

"I guess."

"You guess." I shrug and he mumbles, "Lemme tink—Oh, you mean *da Silva.*" He picks from the population, 250,000, as if it's a baker's dozen.

"Sounds right," I say.

"Dey ain' been Portuguese for three hundred years. Rass boy. Where dat boy live now?" He asks himself, but I think the question's for me.

"In a stucco house." The officer looks at me, tries to discern whether I'm being sarcastic (in which case he should let loose at me), or if I'm a rube (in which case he should fear for my safety). "Its walls kind of slant and there's, well there *was*, a lot of plants and stuff, overgrown. Hydrangea maybe. Those guys weren't very good with hedge clippers."

One of the domino champs interrupts, "Hope dey do better wid da scalpel."

His partners agree. "Yah mon, the gallbladder, she go next Tuesday."

The officer waits.

"There's a black dog next door who just lies behind his pink fence and growls, but he never gets up to run after anything. Seems like he'd get hot—there's not much shade. Seems like he might want to go to the beach. You can walk to the beach; it takes about ten minutes."

"Which beach?" he asks. "Which rasso black dog? You know how many overgrown yards, how many pink fences dis island got?"

"No."

"It just variation on a teeme here girl."

I nod, reminded how repetition unfurls past latitudes.

The domino champions grumble. Their gambler's glow is now streaked with the sweat of the queue. They want to go home, to eat a pepper pot and drink in adulation. "C'mon, fast, fast—ain' goin be no whinin for me if my woman sleep by time I get there," says the bald man.

"Sorry," I say, confused.

The domino gang giggles. "Girl don't even know what whinin means," says the youngest.

"Do too," I pout.

"Whinin is shinin', girl. Makin' love. Sexual inter-course," says the eldest.

"Yeah mon, all de above. An below," says the bald man.

"An side to side Sutra, baby."

"Enough," says the officer. "Which beach?"

"The one with the coconut man."

"*Which* coconut man?"

"Nevermind—I'll get a hotel."

He hands me a card that says *Golden Sand*. "You got cash to pay?" he asks.

I reach into my pocket and deal credit cards like Tarot. Line them before him like fate, like lies.

The smoke from the domino gang is making me swoon, so I ask the eldest for a cigarette. Each draw I take makes me dizzy. I want to lie down on the cool tile underfoot, just spin in place, and not look past customs. Instead, I step out under a sun that swells my eyes, and hail a cab.

I navigate on memory, directing the driver in concentric circles that gradually decrease. All the while I scan for the dog whose address I've forgotten, and squint to spot the slanting house of Tomas through a strangle of hydrangea.

We pass outpost Coca-Cola machines close to the size of the dilapidated shacks that surround them. Both are strung together with a network of wash. Children in plaid uniforms march toward us like belligerent generals. A gated mecca is visible atop a distant hill. I think it was there that Crash stowed me, then sailed to spend time at Turtle Bay, the recording studio where Stones and Sum-ners summered, and Eddy Grant slaved in their shadow.

We drive by and the mecca recedes at a stunning velocity.

At last we round the right neighborhood, a tidy isolation neither kingdom nor dump. The car crawls slow until I see the house, stucco set low behind the haphazard hedges that give it away. I thank the driver for letting me smoke, and dig in my bag for dollars. Instead, I pull up old pound notes. I give them away, and skulk past a growling, graying hound.

The sign on the door says *Do Not Disturb*. I knock. There's no reply, so I peer through a cracked window. The house seems emptied, not just of people, but of furniture and curtains as well. For a moment, I think I have the wrong address or that the boys moved—then I recall sitting cross-legged, and remember that they'd always lived this way. I'm weak and lean against the door for support, but it's unlocked and gives way.

Like some crackpot Goldilocks, I let myself in.

The testosterone smell of unwashed laundry and fermenting dishes greets me. I shut the screen, and sit in the foyer where the air can reach me full-on. I'm trying hard to stay conscious, but my flesh is fidgety and I labor to breathe. Perhaps it's the sleeplessness of the prior evening, or the rapid release of pressure that comes with flight. So many extremes push me toward the edge that I no longer stop to figure out what might be the offender. I lie down, then realize the sight of a fallen woman might alarm the community, so I rise to find the room of Tomas, the wild-eyed, artless Portuguese pirate, who'd begged me to come back, to visit, to marry.

He's the only one of them who's *not* a medical student.

I appraise the clutter: t-shirts, glasses stained with long-drunk juice, and a picture of a brown boy, sipping from a coconut that appears larger than his head. He looks at the camera through indolent doe eyes that strike me with recognition, but I can't tell if they resemble Tomas's—or some other long-ago beau's. I look again, but can't be sure, then as I circle the room in a final sweep for anatomy books I collapse on an enormous futon, flat to the floor, and swallow a handful of drugs—the last of my prescription.

But it's too late. Destruction rattles through my blood like Amtrak. I can feel my body surge with its own insubstantiality—my mind floats on the bloat of nothingness. My lips balloon, my eyes swell shut, and I strain through slits to see my thighs alight in patterns; purple, once dull, has now become dahlia. My histine-laden mast cells burgeon out of control, releasing pigments with a display of pyrotechnic intensity. I panic with presentiment and plead for the attack to stop, no longer out of fear but in embarrassment. I want to at least speak with my holiday acquaintance before fainting on his floor. I zag drunkenly to the medicine cabinet and find a large bottle of liquid antihistamine, cut in a lead glass intricacy. The weight of it wobbles in my shaking hand. I admire the quality of flagon and make a mental note to fill it with hydrangea for the boys when I'm through. Is that wax upon its cap, I wonder—and are colds really so common here? Will this viscous red do the trick—provide me another installment of breath, lend me a little, just a day, just a grain, of time?

Just then everything goes white. No time left to think about a reaction with the pills I swallowed. Down the hatch—I drink until all that's left is a bloodstained prism.

Through my anaphylactic fog I glimpse a beacon of reprieve. Then I pass out.

The time is now. The safehouse I've escaped to sits on a shore. I shuffle through sand, but the house becomes distant and the walk back is long—I look up to see the ocean on fire.

My uncle has been watching the house from afar and I go to him.

"Do you think it's a coincidence?" I say.

"I have trouble remembering," he says.

I tell him I saw his wife a few months back.

Again, he says he doesn't remember.

"Don't remember?" I say.

"Uh-uh."

"You lived with her," I press.

"Oh yeah—she was cute."

I find this comment strange since he'd once risked his life for her. Then I realized he was dead. And it all made sense.

Feet. The feet of men my smelling salts.

Twenty hours later, I'm awakened by the unmistakable stench of feet. And refreshed by the must of damp swim trunks. A tall bearded youth flips anxiously through the Physician's Desk Reference. Tomas stands beside him and stares blankly at me. *Yes, of course,* green *eyes, my favorite.* I smile. The oldest student, fittingly the closest to being a doctor, explodes in rage. He shakes with disapproval, spews expletives in Bajan, then pulls himself together to address me. "How mucha dis you take?" he asks.

"A lot."

"Doncha know, dread girl, dat if you die here it look mighty bad—dead American girl in a houseful o men, mighty bad."

More expletives.

"You take enough a ten men." Aside to Tomas he asks, "You like she? Mon you crazy mon." Then to me, "What you do a ting like dat for?"

"I *needed* a lot. I was trying to save myself, not kill myself." I realize with gratitude that here they're scared of incarceration, not paisley.

Also, the boys have a better grasp of the affliction than my own plodding practitioners. They take me to a clinic, where I'm injected with what looks to be a nineteenth-century needle. The East Indian doctor immediately names the disease that has taken Americans over a year to identify, but this diagnosis causes him such distress that he urges me to return to the States for treatment.

At the local pharmacist, whispers are exchanged and I'm given stronger refills of my prescriptions. When I whine (not the whinin Tomas had hoped for), they throw in a large bottle of Danish antihistamine.

I stay in the company of men for less than a week. I sleep, I sweep, I do some dishes. But think it's best not to beleaguer the bewildered any longer than necessary. I crave solitude and Tomas deserves his own bed. Still, he's up in arms over my leaving; claims the town will ridicule him over the loss of his "girlfriend." That ridicule comes not from my illness or appearance, but because of my *dis*appearance, is touching—notwithstanding the macho implications. I promise no embarrassment will befall him. To save face, I assure Tomas that I'll tell anyone who asks that he'd tired of me. A certain surreality has followed my lapse of consciousness and as seductive, as perversely exhilarating as this tropical Peyton Place is, I must move.

⌇

I open the unlocked door, skirt the inert dog—and start walking. I walk past houses until there is only pavement, palm trees, and, every so often, food stands. I stop to rest at the foot of an incline, and an old woman from out of nowhere taps my shoulder and asks if she can have a ride up the coast. I tell her I don't have a car, but I'm on my way to get one. We walk to a rental agency, where I discover I can't get a car, that the expense will eat up my fast-dwindling credit like barracuda to guppy—so I settle for a moke, a sort of Australian golf cart with a lawn mower engine. My card is charged and the agent is nice enough to forward me $100 bd. I don't know how much, if any, credit I have left.

The woman and I rumble up the coast, until we come to the grocer where she shops (her own credit will never run out). I offer to wait, but she refuses and sends me north to an off-season oceanography station where, if I don't mind sharing everything but my bed, I can stay a while. I drop her beside the road, but before I can thank her she's gone.

I go north, and take a tiny room on the shore of St. James. It is a pocket of asceticism sandwiched between Britain's bloodlines and glitterati.

Now I'm a recluse on a coast. I look closely at its line and know the trick will be not to avert my gaze. If I can navigate such unstable sands, there's the chance I'll go mad marking endless recursions. And I wonder—if my thousand and one steps equate two of true forward motion. And if forward is really that.

I hold tight to my Danish antihistamine, and throw my steroids, harbingers of stasis, into the sea. Free from palliatives, I sense the motion of a new life, but know neither its direction nor duration.

I exist, for the first time, in my immediate surroundings, which are ever-changing, infinite. Within the near corners of my room, a lamp of smoked glass glows a radius that barely reaches the slim, single bed beside it. Cracks crawl the walls like vines, interrupted only by bubbles or peeling where the smell of yellow stinks like virus. I sweat and sip at my glass of water while the room pulsates with transience. At night, the distant repetition of drums thrash and poke an old self toward exit while outside rain streams relentless from the sky, able to both paint the fury long held back and wash it from within. Rest comes easily. Each night I go no fewer than sixteen hours to the dark sleep that drags one through narrow dyslexic hallways—a sleep to long for, that seems to come only with drugs, sickness, or natural disasters.

I awake slimed and stronger to see new progress on the pointillism of mildew that surrounds me.

Dispatches from the old life arrive in pieces—but my interpretation of them changes. I spend my days *like water*, I hear my brother say. I rise only to boil a pot of rice, or fetch from the communal shelf a torn paperback, its pages missing in clumps—the narrative more credible this way. I gather tiny bananas the islanders call figs, and as I reach high for them, I notice white spots in painless design sprayed atop my paisley. It is as if I'm being peeled out. In my Caribbean dengue a world rots in time with myself; the syncopation of decay lulls me.

"Muggy," my mother had always called such weather. In the southern September twilight, she repeated the word over and over. It sounded dirty to me then, like soiled underwear, worn again, inside out. Now my underwear lies in piles with black-dotted shifts and rank t-shirts. I leave such garments about to waft gloriously. The scent of impermanence reassures me. My books are untouched, the peanut butter unopened.

I mourn my dog. But three others, seemingly stray, guard me. Poppy and Woof, misplaced Newfoundlands, and Jaws, a wiry retriever of unknown origin. Each morning while Poppy fends off the lumbering advances of soft-headed Woof, Jaws and I swim. My skin is simultaneously healed by the salt sea and clawed by Jaws's floundering. In the afternoons, the old woman I'd taken to the grocer, who belongs to the dogs, comes to me with apologies for their intrusion (which I fend off with gratitude) and fish sandwiches (which I buy for a dollar). I'm happy to see her, but not surprised. Again and again, she feeds me— appreciative of appreciation. I eat greasy fish balls and mustard cheese sandwiches, chicken when I'm lucky; wash it down with Coca-Cola and Banks beer.

"Where are you from?" she asks.

"Nowhere." It's enough for her. I say I've been ill and she assures me my newly acquired white spots are a harmless fungus. She says she can mix a special tincture for it. I refuse, but let her treat old wounds. She rubs unripe papaya on my skin, erasing the worst. I begin to sit on the beach for short intervals.

My paisley no longer scares off intruders so I wear a moldering leather bikini to fend off the vegans that have drifted from a nearby resort to encroach on my plot of sand. Blood bubbles have become ineffectual bruises that now seem to me decorative, dim in their offense among the tiresome tattoos: flowers, hearts, and pentagrams that populate the parade of ankles I watch from ground level. Occasionally something interesting catches my eye, and I rue the lack of blank space on my own flesh. But it's the scars relegated to women that strike me most. They are neat and surgically savage, just beneath the armpits of women, some barely twenty, linear scars that lack my own designs. I stare at the matter pushed inside, taut against skin at unnatural angles, and wonder what they feel like. I bow toward my own stainless breasts, and shudder at the thought of such violation.

The rains lessen, and the world is still, so still I can hear my bones speak. In this stillness comes a freedom, born of disregard. This winter, Death passes like a dog. She seeks to find some quick movement, a scuffle of escape, to smell fear, but can sense only the mildewing rot of my surroundings. And so Death, disinterested, lopes up and over the island, down the Atlantic coast, and takes half of a honeymooning couple, who had been repeatedly warned about the tide.

I've been here before, too. But time, and a scant jog of geography renders an island unrecognizable. Where once I'd stayed in jacuzzied resorts now I've strayed to a hut, sans plumbing. And cuisine at Joseph's by the boat slip has shifted to cheese sandwiches by the Papaya Queen.

I'm curious about the change, so I walk back to the scene of my long-ago holiday: south, to the Christ Church rental villa where I had, out of vagary, lain with Tomas on a replacement of its pristine carpet, an immaculate imitation flown in from Belgium to replace the ruined Persian— a casualty of Crash's bash. He'd called a week before from some faraway gig and made me smile as I'd sprawled on our bed, Pig at its foot, like some great squatty sphinx. "Let's go off," he said, "to our own special island, somewhere near Tahiti, let's just meet there right now." (Thirty hours in the air was nothing to Crash.)

"How about Barbados?" I'd said.

The record company paid him to throw a party there, "for Bajan musicians," they'd said. "Everyone can jam, in a celebration of cross-cultural camaraderie." The company knew, as do the world's most successful musicians, that there are no copyright laws in the Caribbean.

Jagger and Jerry didn't come to the party, but their child's nanny, Delia, did. She wore a black leather mini and a pair of thigh-high boots, the heels of which (seven-inch spikes) raised her to the eye-level of the young man she addressed. I listened to them from inside the doors that separated us.

"I don't like their music, Tomas, do you?" The musicians played a Sparrow cover. *I am not a soca man.* . . .

"It not *der* music—it from a Trini mon name Sparrow—Mighty Sparrow."

"That's a silly name. So, d'ya like him?" She danced in spite of herself. Her long legs, anchored by spikes to the garden ground, swayed in perfect time.

"Yes . . . well . . . I like he some. But he ol' mon—da Frank Sinatra of da Caribbean. I radder lissen Pink Floyd. What about you—I guess you like da Stones," he said, then slumped against the breadfruit tree.

"*What?* Talk about old, no way." She wiggled, using all of her tall-glass-of-water body to make waves. But Tomas didn't notice; he was looking at me. "I rather fancy Madonna, 'cause you can't dance to Pink Floyd," said Delia.

"Mm," I said, then turned away. Crash had just finished a tour with Madonna. He'd sent me a round-trip ticket to the States when I'd begged to go. "One week, no Willa," he said. I'd been inspired by Madonna's smarts and success. I soon became ashamed. America's number one performer paid her warm-up act next to nothing, then sentenced them to silence. Tours are to sell records, so, in effect, she'd cost Crash America.

At RFK Stadium, I'd sized her up: She was symmetry itself. But small. Very small. She reproached me with a smile she made by biting down hard; her magenta lips formed a sine wave—the high, a sneer, the low, condescension. "I still don't think she knows who I am," said Crash.

"Oh, she knows exactly who you are."

Cultural Exhaust were a benign bunch. Perfect for the vamp to tramp on. She even disallowed visible billing. The ticket typeface she chose was so large that there was only room for her own name—artful in its christianity. Nobody knew who the opening act was, so the one time they were allowed to play, the crowd didn't show until the end of their set. She usually spent the afternoons yelling at her crew so their sound check took the place of Cultural Exhaust's sound. Without shows they had nothing to do, but this boredom brought Crash and me closer—our age span shrank. Everyone becomes a child under such constraint. Think snow days, shutdowns, roadside breakdowns, smokes and stories and snuggles.

We'd clambered beneath the stage to watch her rehearsal with a mixture of horror and entertainment. Before us a deluded dominatrix with visions of Marilyn straddled RFK with an interminable endurance. When the show was over we went to dinner.

The chef made traditional English dishes for the boys, but I couldn't weather Wellington, so I'd wished aloud, "Is there anything else?"

"Do you like fish?" the chef said. I could've kissed him. There stood an industrial plate carrier stacked with seafood. Too good to be true. He pulled one out for me.

"Are you sure you won't be one short for the crew?" I said.

"Oh no, that's not for the crew, that's all for our star."

"My goodness, how *does* she stay so svelte?"

"Aw, she hardly eats at all, just likes to have a selection of her selection."

"Well thanks. I appreciate it. Just can't seem to keep any more meat down."

"Aw, no problem," he said, and I sat down to salmon with hollandaise. I didn't even mind when Marquis, the bass player, began to complain about Sean Penn.

"He spat at me again; he can really muster some loogies," Marq said with some admiration. "Guess it comes from all those pints."

I felt ill. Lit another cigarette.

Marq hacked. "You've got one going."

"Are you all finished?" the chef interrupted. We shrugged simultaneously.

"Sure," said Ted.

"Yeah," said Marq.

"Why?" Crash asked, not quite through building castles with his potatoes.

"She wants to eat now."

Madonna pushed past us on her way in, then slammed the door before us. We could hear her halfway down the hall. This time we didn't have to sneak—her cry was deafening.

"Who ate my goddamn fish?!"

I leaned on the vacant bark of breadfruit tree, next to Tomas. "I like Sinatra."

"Sinatra can't even remember he own lyrics mon."

"That's okay," I said, "I'll remember them for him." I neglected to mention that I remember little else in life *but* lyrics.

"Floyd's new album *is* awesome," I conceded.

"Your cod fritter is great," said Tomas. I nodded and thanked him; I didn't tell him that nothing there was mine.

They were the only partygoers near my age, and Delia did remind me a bit of Willa, who'd hung posters of Andy Gibb, while I hid pictures in my mind, of Mick and his lips.

Delia wrinkled her little snub nose, under my scrutiny. "You look gorgeous," I told her.

"Thank you," she said, and beamed. Her snub sank into an expanse of a blemish-free complexion.

We basked briefly in our current of misdirected compliments, until Delia nudged Tomas and jerked her head back toward the inside, where a towering man, in suit, sandals, and socks, fed on roast goat straight from the steam table—all the time focused on Delia and me. He had sunglasses on, but you could tell he was staring by the way his body turned to face us when we shifted; he moved in closer, like metal to the pull of our gamin poles. "Rasso man," Tomas muttered, then excused himself. I saw Tomas speaking to Crash, who, minutes later, asked the man to leave. The man, whom I've secretly dubbed "Monarch," did so with a smile.

"Jealous?" I asked Crash hopefully, when he came by with a magnum for refills.

"Whassit?" He lingered over the nanny's flute.

"You kicked out that creep who was staring at us," I

strained over the din of a hundred partygoers, and signaled like the umpire I appeared to be in the black-and-white Vivienne Westwood that Crash had insisted on.

"He was? Oh—I hadn't noticed. Sorry luv, I'm sorry." Crash quaffed from the bottle.

"He's creepy," said Delia.

"I'm with ya babe," I said. "Why *did* you kick him out?" I asked Crash.

"Bloody drug dealer," he said under his breath.

"Wha? He didn't *hug* Delia?"

"Whassit?" Music wasn't the only obstacle to our communication; the sounds from the swarm disoriented as well. And although most of the guests were Anglos, their speech sounded alien, flopped, like dialogue translated into a foreign language, then back again to English.

The Bajans switched to soca, and someone turned the stereo to acid jazz; the roar of mixed musics rattled the villa. I mouthed wide, talked loud. Crash interrupted what he couldn't hear. "They say he was trying to make it snow." He answered my question in his politic manner, with an idiom unknown to the climate.

The day after the party Tomas was at our door. I apologized for my appearance. "Hangovers are hell in the heat," I said.

"Then why do you drink so much?"

"I lose track of losing track," I confessed. "So what'd ya forget?"

"What?"

"Nevermind. What d'ya know about that big guy, the one Crash kicked out?"

"He's Bajan man, went to Harvard," Tomas said, then

changed the subject. "Kelly Slater's goin surf Bathsheba tomorrow. Wanna go?" I wasn't sure if I was thrilled, or taken aback by his brazenness.

"Who's Kelly Slater?"

"He from da States—best surfer in da world!" he said, incredulous.

His interest intrigued me. He knew Crash lived with me; he'd seen that last night. Then I realized Tomas wasn't looking for a duel—it was his strength of observation that had brought him here. He knew that Crash was rarely home; he'd seen that, too.

"Sure," I said. "Why not."

Tomorrow came, but not Bathsheba. We never made it out of the house; we made it on the carpet.

The following morning Crash brought me tea on the terrace. He still made tea, and ran my bath, when he was around. I took more showers then; it was too hot for baths, anyway. Crash thought the singe of rug along my back was sunburn. "You should spend more time inside," he said, before leaving for lunch at the Jaggers.

The lapping lulls me toward stasis, so with Jaws at my heels, I put on my sneakers—a pair of tattered Converses whose color cannot be named, a hue like the confluence at St. Lucy, neither blue nor green but something between these east and west waters—and with them, I walk south. The soles are coming loose and I realize that going shod can be more perilous than barefoot. I take them off, this favorite pair that has been with me since before Crash. The attention they'd attracted varied. Sometimes I was ridiculed for their once-bright color. When I accompanied Crash to a gig in Scandinavia, their canvas shone against the white of snow like a quetzal too far off course. "That—that is good joke," a red-faced Finn had said to us and pointed—to my sneakers, I'd thought, but now I think maybe he was referring to the match before him.

I keep walking. I have no idea how far—sand slows time so. But it's easier to maneuver my way through now that my feet are bare. I feel my calves ache and can't imagine how one runs on such a surface. Past a certain point Jaws will no longer follow me. She doesn't whine, but simply drops behind. She's unsentimental about letting go.

I walk farther. I don't know where I'm going, only the direction: south. The sand is deserted until it's not, until I come to a place where lounge chairs scatter, reclining apart from one another. Women stiff with couture occupy a few—their pose makes them look as if they're undergoing a CAT scan. Some of the other women mill about knee-deep in water, looking beneath the blue as if for lost treasure, but they see only the same smooth stones beneath their feet. No one swims. I notice that the only men around are starched servants who hurry to refill tea glasses. Come four o'clock I'll bet the refreshments get stronger.

When I approach, the women freeze as if in a Robbe-Grillet production. All beaches in Barbados are public, yet the servants eye me with disdain. I keep walking, but the brush that soon blocks my way is difficult to get through—too difficult for the public. Although I'm covered by a loose long-sleeved dress, it scratches my skin with a crosshatch of welts. Then a jowled man puts his tray of cucumber sandwiches down and confronts me with considerably more irritation. He shows me the way out—up the hill and through the front door of the hotel.

I continue south. I pass a few food stands before making my way back to the beach, but, out of loyalty to the Papaya Queen, I don't buy.

Next there's a Shakey's serving pineapple pizza—a frightening thought. But their fried chicken isn't advertised—nothing can beat island chicken.

I realize I've ventured farther from my patch of sand than I'd expected to; I look up to see men surround a coconut tree that stretches endless toward the sun and realize I've come close to where I began.

The men speak singsong as they sell their coconut water. I think I recognize the words of Shelley, or Keats, in "the fate of the coconut husk to float . . ." but before I can be sure, they stifle their verse. They hesitate, like children on a hot day who suddenly stop spouting water on each other because an elder, unappreciative of such pleasure, approaches.

Or perhaps their silence comes because I have clothed myself too well before men almost naked.

"Ay—you—Britain Wurse Invesmont." It takes me a while to understand, then I grin. "BWIA," it's imprinted across the plastic bag I carry my sneakers and towel in. I loosen my grip and the colors lift onto my hand in backward script.

"It's good for you," he says, passing me a coconut. I take it and taste. *Gross*—like sugared dishwater. I don't leave, though; I want to stay and share shade beneath the towering palms of the coconut men's sanctuary. The fronds stretch over us like great prehistoric ferns. On the island, time is not evident in leaves, but lies obscured in roots. Above, there is no gradient. Just split-second change— from dry to wet, dark to light. The slide of a redundant sun onto ever-lit greenery marks the day. Here, time's arrow gyrates.

The coconut men are fixed in their Eden, but the food stand across a blacktop road blows smoke, seducing me with its scent. I smell coffee and imagine brushing its brown velvet liquid, heady with unwashed cane and sweet evaporated milk, across my tongue—then I anticipate a rush (if I'm lucky enough to arrive before the pot becomes cold and acrid with neglect) of dancing heat. The taint of coconut brew is washed away. I bid the men good day, and change direction, just a stone's throw, across the glittering blacktop road.

I order no food, just a coffee—strong and sharp and cheap. I put spoon after spoon of golden stuck sugar into my cup and sit and sip. A girl I think I've seen before looks up from across a cracked sea of plastic blue, tables upon which spilt sugar makes glutinous whitecaps. I'm dizzied. She has a smile like a pat on the back. Her dress is stylish, conservative, and snug against a lithe body that reaches so far it's as if she'll tower over me. But when she gets up I see that she's the same height as myself, if not shorter. She glides through openings, traversing the narrow breaks between us, and as she comes closer I realize she's a tour guide. I'd seen her, saddled by the ridiculous Brits, at the airport, on my most recent arrival.

She tells me her name is Marcia. She pronounces this *Mar-see-ya.* "I haven't seen you around," she says. I realize that she is stuck between feelings toward me. At one pole lies the easily procured adventure of a tourist, the other pulls her closer to a girl whose brightness, like her hair, her shoes, has been washed out. She stares at the strange tendrils that peek from beneath my unseasonable tunic, then asks outright about the paisley. When I tell her I've been ill, she offers me a cigarette. I take a Silk Cut, and remember they're my favorite—though I'd smoked Dunhills because Crash supplied them free. She's darker than most of the islanders, and I wonder if she spends her days in the sun. Her eyes are black and sloe, she has a small upturned fairy nose. Her cheekbones are precipitous; they could hurt someone. She tells me she's originally from Guyana, and I think of thousands sipping cyanide from paper cups, think of the Arawak, the incomprehension of such complete and rapid extinction. And coffee—I think of coffee—sweet, sharp, electric. "Where are you from?" she asks.

"Nowhere," I answer. But it's not enough. She eyes me with reproof. And I, guilty, focus on the sand beneath me, and begin, with my white-fungused toenails, to dig.

"C'mon, remember, you must be from someplace."

"Nowhere."

"Remember . . ." she insists.

"The States," I say.

"You don't look American," she says. "You look Trini." I know that this means everything, a great melt of east and west, and I know the country has been raped by both of its riches. And that Miss World is from Trinidad this year. It's not a bad year to look Trini.

I like this identity as much as any other. There have been many. Because my behavior is, to my mother, erratic and unfathomable, she insists that, unlike herself, I'm Israeli, that she shared a hospital room with an Israeli woman and they were each given the wrong child. I know the women there are soldiers, so I've often thought of myself as a warrior born too far from my country.

"I've never been there, to Trinidad," I say.

"You will go," she insists, "I'm sure of it."

I believe her, and panic. Suddenly I see there's no place for me to latch on to. I see nothing that does not shift. Just sea beyond, and sand beneath, that I dig with my feet, in evasion. With each scoop more sand slides in. In sand each step forward is halved. Still I dig. I dally in this calculus, like a guilty child, the kind that loathes chronology. But there's no way out, and I waste what, in the end, is the upset of an egg timer. *I can well understand why children love sand.*

I stutter silence and ask for another cigarette; she seems to understand my evasion. She's a sophisticate, a clever ruse, a tropical Holly Golightly—I feel plain and awkward near her. "That's a pretty dress," she says. It is an odd piece of clothing, blotched with pill balls, partially eaten. It feels good against me.

We smoke some more. It burns my throat, and travels down to expand in my chest, soldering torn tissue with fire. Or so I believe. And so I perk up. Marcia flashes her white pat-on-the-back, and I'm compelled to compliment her teeth. She says it's because she gets them cleaned so often, that dentistry is supplied here to anyone who wants it. I tell her that in America it's not. But she already knows this, as the coconut men know Keats and Shelley, as the Papaya Queen knows how to heal. Then, as if to console, she tells me a realer reason—a child's bus ride to school—travels spent sucking sugar cane, peeling it, pulling the husks back. Nothing can make teeth stronger than sugar cane. She asks if I wish to attend a celebration this week. It will be a "fête," she says gloriously. "There will be cricket and polo. We can go there together." I ask her what the celebration is for, and she answers as if I already knew, but had simply forgotten.

"Why, Independence Day, of course."

To get to the fairgrounds I catch a bus, hell from its driver for too large a bill, and fleas from the dog beside me. But the view from my destination is worth it. The party seems to stretch past the horizon, an ever-burgeoning body of brown skin and ivory clothes. Children hold hands and run, an undulating, unending clothesline of wash. Against the dusk, the entire sight seems sepia, as if mine is a vision borrowed from the dead. They say that angels see thus— this landscape before me in brilliant bichrome. Maybe it's real, maybe it's Mount Gay.

I've been drinking rum and lime for hours waiting for Marcia, who finally, at seven or so, arrives with the same man I'd seen naked earlier that day.

When I'd gone to pick her up at his address, she'd shushed me upon entrance, and her eyes beamed silent giggles. My loose white cotton, more djellaba than jumpsuit, passed inspection, but she handed me a nail scissor and emery board, glaring in demand that I remove such transgression. I cut, dropping soiled nails, long and flat like platypus bills left too long in the mud, and sanded under her direction. Then she dragged me into the bedroom, winked, and pointed in introduction. Across the bed lay sprawled a young body, lean and lengthy, the color of caramel. His hair, cast a lighter caramel by the sun, veiled sleeping eyes. His member slept too, reclining like a satiate sea horse across a quadricep damp from exertion. I panicked, thinking he might awaken from the intensity of our observation. But I didn't want to insult my hostess with a rejection of her offering. I still wasn't sure as to the extent of her offering... but as she drew me from the room, I saw Marcia as the Avon lady of vital makeovers, and took the interlude as a kind of free sample. See you soon she said, then shoved me out the door with a map to the fairgrounds and a tube of red lipstick.

The naked man, now clothed, turns out to be a docile Canadian, a university professor here on some quest to save the sea turtles. I don't know why they're in such danger, but recall a morning spent keeping Jaws from gnawing a huge overturned turtle in its death throes. When I went back later that afternoon to bury it, it was gone. I wondered about the disappearance of such immensity—one hundred years gone to soup.

"Marcia has told me a lot about you," the man says. I wonder at the extent of her wisdom, so well hidden from myself—but because I'm drunk I think more about slowness, how it can stretch a species to eras, or leave it open to instant destruction. So I ask.

"Is it true about them, the turtles? That they know what killed the dinosaurs?" I struggle to confine my gaze to his eyes, eyes that had, until this moment, remained unseen. They are both knowing and harmless. Uncommon. I wonder if his body works as his eyes. If within my own eyes spins my blood, veering others away with a glance before they near my body, a vessel struck by a thousand visible storms, from the mind's eye of which I see the eyes of family, softened by pity, the eyes of Crash, vulgar with fear. I hear him sing the blues—*I got blood in my eyes for you baby, blood in my eyes for you.* I can't stand to see any more with my own eyes; the world I admired now turns my stomach, then, suddenly, spins out of sight. I don't know whether I'm glad to be rid of it; I wonder if I'll die swift, not sickly, of alcohol poisoning, wonder if all turtles are tortoises, but before I can guess any of these things, I smell the medicine-smell of undigested rum pour from my body onto the professor's shoes. Then I pass over and away toward a vision of Dali's *Argus*—and I claw at its canvas with unmanicured nails.

When I come to there's a fire in the distance burning an effigy of the queen. I stretch and look for corgies. A man I don't know hands me a Coca-Cola, and I feel Marcia reach to smooth my hair. The professor sits shoeless beside her, looking slightly winded, and I wonder if they've been dancing or if I've missed another free sample.

The darkness is iridescent. Women in the crowd have switched to evening attire, golds and glints and sequins— in the distance they surround the burning queen like fire-flies. The band plays soca. Couples grind, separate, then return to their perfect meld. Lone dancers move their hips in a figure eight. "Old-folks music," the children say, and wait until the drone of western pop to dance.

I shimmy a little to both. I feel remarkably good—I'm hungry. I sip the soda slowly, disappointed by its dilute-ness. Again I'm handed sustenance by the man I don't know. This time it's chicken. Big bus–riding, fat food–snatching, children-pecking, island chicken. There's no better bird than the island chicken. I finish a breast and start on the leg. Then I snatch a sip of Marcia's martini (she's brought her own pitcher) and realize I'm still drunk. I give back the drink, but not before I've eaten the olive.

The man I don't know stares down at me; now I think that I have seen him before on the beach. Running boats, or perhaps it was sailboards. His body is roped and less massive than it appears, but what distinguishes him is his color, a deep brown, salted and cured—like jerky. He's young but you have to get up close to see his youth. He is the oldest young person I've ever seen. He has an authority about him, and I wonder for a moment if I'm under arrest.

"Peter Rock, this is my friend," Marcia says.

"Sorry for she," Peter says.

"Hey Bashful, say thanks for the chicken," the professor yawns.

"Oh, thanks," I say. "Is Rock really your surname?"

Peter only shakes his head, the look from beneath his brow tells me to halt any further inquiry.

"Everyone calls him Peter Rock, always." Marcia continues to provoke him. "His real last name is Van—" but Peter slams down his beer, his eyes wild in rage, and Marcia relinquishes.

"He's against identity," I tell her as he turns to go.

"Half Dutch, half Trini," she says. "He's been watching you sleep. I . . . I guess he likes you." She seems just as puzzled by this as me. "Just be careful." I sense that Peter is an uninvited variable in the equation that Marcia wishes me to solve.

"It's my presence, my paisley," I say, "it incites such uncertainty." But already she's gone too—I spot her dancing with the others—awash in a sea of glitter and fire.

Peter brings back more chicken and sits closer, then he smiles for the first time this evening. "Why haven't you been past my part of the beach lately?" he asks.

"I was in a rut," I answer, "thought I should change direction."

"But you ain't even warm de path." He *was* the man I'd seen. I remember then that I'd thought him rough, his hair too unkempt. I suspected he smelled. Now, up close, his only waft is the aseptic, near-imperceptible scent of salt. I'm flattered that he looked for me—my instinct is to return the compliment by addressing him by name. So instead, I ask, "You wanna dance?" But he just shakes his head, his hair wriggling like snakes in flight. No, Peter does not dance; Peter just sits still, his eyes hoarding snapshots, looking, looking at me sitting still. I yawn, and he says that he'll take me home. I hesitate . . . but . . . I really don't want to wait for Marcia and the professor, nor do I want to take a bus—if there is a bus at this hour. I suspect walking will take a long time, and am certain that finding my way home alone will be more difficult, more dangerous, than with Peter. So I concede.

"Stay put—right here," Peter warns. Minutes later he rides up on a Harley 1000 and tells me to get on. I wonder if Tomas or his medical student friends are around. I haven't thought about this for a while, but I do bear the burden of Tomas's manhood. Absurd, I think; still, I owe him and the respect of ritual seems such a small concession.

"I'll meet you out front by the gates," I tell Peter. He's insulted by the implication.

"Get on, dread girl," he growls. But I don't. He rides off in a squeal of dirt and exhaust. *Oh well*. With my obligations in hand, I start walking. When I get to the gate Peter is there, waiting. I tell him about Tomas and his scowl turns to a grandfather smile. He lifts me onto his bike—in a moment we've hit the sound wall and I'm screaming unheard into the night. We pass the turn to my hut, safe under the watch of hounds, and continue north.

"Where are we going?" I yell into his ear.

"Hold tight," he says. The bike speeds up and I imagine myself splat on the road, my swirls unfurled in a rush of caustic blood. We go north, dip and turn through Spring Garden—the brief roundabout that Bajans call Highway. *Let we go, NOW, Spring Garden Highway.* The lyrics loop insistent, until the rush of open road drowns them out. We head straight for St. Lucy, the island pinnacle, the point of conflux. We skid through Blackrock, and do wheelies through Holetown. I settle into the thrill of motion, the bike strong between my legs. My screams of terror have turned to delight.

We slow somewhere west of his namesake, St. Peter. Speightown, probably—near St. Lucy, but not quite. We pull up beside a house that in the dark seems more an extended car park. It's much squatter than most of the one-stories that make up the island, and I half expect a gnome to peep from its shutters, but instead there comes a cacophony of barking, the cry of dogs alert to their master's presence, but aware still of an intruder.

"Quiet," Peter demands; the dogs half whimper, then stop. He opens the door and lets them out; they're beautiful animals, Dobermans sleek with a life of exercise and fresh fish. They come to sniff me, and Peter warns not to pet them. They nose their heads beneath my hands. I sense that perhaps Peter's warning is a ploy to hoard attention for, as well as to instill reliance upon, himself.

"Vicious curs, huh?" I say.

"What curse?" he asks.

"Nevermind," I say.

"*Dat* a curse girl, dat no kinda word for you. You keep saying dat word, your blood run thin."

"Oh," I say as if struck.

"Now don't go get scare—dogs dey sense it," he warns.

"Mmm, I'm sure they do," I say and scratch their ears, then follow him inside to the kitchen where he places the dog dishes, big as bull's heads, atop the counter. "Can I help feed them?" I ask. He sees this as an overly aggressive move—and marches me to the bedroom. There's no furniture, just a mattress on the floor surrounded by stacks of videos: Spencer Tracy's *Dr. Jekyll and Mr. Hyde*, Hepburn's *Bringing Up Baby*, and lots of Steve McQueen. There's also a vcr, a rather large set that appears to be not a television but simply a monitor, and a camcorder eyeing me from its mount. I stare back, and cap it. "I want to go home," I say.

"Not tonight." He shuts the door, but doesn't lock it. I sit down on the edge of the mattress to peruse his collection, but am distracted by the coolness of the sheets beneath me; they smell of sun and salt breeze. I stew but before I have time to boil Peter is seated beside me on the large mattress on the floor. He takes his shirt off in a single swift motion, and lies down beside me. I can hear the panting of dogs outside beneath the shutters. I can't risk revealing my scars; again I say that I want to go home. I speak in the direction of Peter, but look the other way.

When he bows his head my eyes wash over him, each fiber polished from motion, a great melding of curves, a convergence of convex and concave. I stare at the dip that precedes the shorts he's kept on, the trail leading beneath them.

He reaches for me.

I catch my breath and hold it; he holds me so tightly I find it hard to exhale. Beneath my petrified flesh, I feel the uncertain motion of an aquifer, resisting and wanting. I don't know what to do, so I panic and reach for his shorts—not really remembering if this is correct.

He holds my hand, senses its qualm, then moves it away.

Although I'm dressed, my splotches removed from sight, I ask him if my marks bother him.

He remains silent.

If he watched me on the beach he must have seen them, darkening a little each day with the sun, its light coaxing their pigment-laden cells to etch darker what had begun to fade. Should I press on or just succumb to the fact that I'm more walking symbol of time and space than woman, a half-ghost next to a breathing man on a moonless night?

"You don't want this," Peter says, and pulls away from me.

"I don't know," I say, and ask for a cigarette.

"Smoke is bad." He reaches round my neck, and sweeps my hair, snarled by the ride, atop my head. He unzips me and the white cotton falls like an outgrown husk. I bow toward my hips and see that scars have made stars of the new shiny skin, pressed taut against my stolen tissue. Peter presses his face to my back and runs his hands lightly over unmarked breasts, then speaks into me. "Jah press hard when he form you—maybe kiss too hard. Anyway, Grandma say she wash dem 'way."

The Papaya Queen, gossiping without me. Peyton Place. "News don' lack a carrier," I say. It's her favorite expression.

"Don' dig nuttin' babe," he says. "You really want to

go home?" I think that this may be the longest disquisition I'll hear from him in our acquaintance, and in gratitude, and because I *do* want to be here, I say no, ashamed that I'd thought the only "honor" worth defense was my own. That a male body was meant to do tricks under the vaguest of circumstance. Peter pulls me down beside him and tells me we should get to sleep before "the blue."

The term jars me; "blue" was Crash's word for dawn, but there's no fear in Peter's voice when he speaks it. *Meanings migrate like lemmings and words kill. . . .* I once heard an author say. If Crash was awake at dawn he would scream like a crazed vampire about the horror of what he called "the blue." He hated to be awake when the passage of time was hung up to dry, but his life as a musician deemed that sometimes a job was unfinished until such dread hour—he resented this beyond any corporeal description—it was as if he were forced to see his life ripped from him.

But as Peter drifts to sleep, I lay in wait for the blue; remain there in his arms and dare the blue to touch me.

Independence Day recedes and the sun comes glowing above the horizon, an astonishing curveball that strikes me with possibility. I lift my face to meet its warmth; stretch to keep it there.

My moke can't take the hills, so after a number of near-tragic climbs, I trade it in for a motorcycle—light enough to *pick up if it should go down* (as Peter instructed). I'm glad to see the golf cart go. I save money on the trade-in, and buy some time. Two months of transit turns into three. Each day, I ride farther. Peter's arrival, at what might be my end, unsettled me. I wanted him, but sought my self. The former was so easy, the latter, a travail.

It took me a good half hour over rough terrain to reach the ocean. I feared a blow-out on the scarcely inhabited west side, and, sometimes, drove too carefully. But I always sped up past the lost colonies of Caucasian settlers, their minds and bodies weakened by a self-imposed exclusion that had led gradually to ostracism. Long ago, a group of prosperous farmers had refused contact with Africans, and the others who'd embraced them. The remnants of this St. Joseph plantation, where brother had slept with sister, are referred to as the "spa." It's a spooky island interstice, where hunger strikes and dirty children play like tired old women. The brown the whites had resisted is now caked upon them as if in penance; pale faces gape from beneath filth, witless from implosion.

There was some relief, though, in reaching this unsettling landmark; it heralded the great interregnum of the Atlantic.

The wild west coast is now overrun with surfers. So, solitude squashed, I sit between interlopers, and watch teams from all over the world practice. But the "Americans" have not yet arrived.

They descend at three A.M., the day of the competition, appearing suddenly in a bar where Chilean coaches sit and sip to calm their pre-competition jitters. I'm there, too, eating free pretzels and cod balls—salt food to up the drink bills, but I don't buy. I'd waited on the beach until after dark, to reclaim my unobstructed view of the waves. I guess I lost track of time. The "Americans" order shots, they're already drunk from the flight and coked up to boot. My countrymen slur and spit. I leave the bar ashamed.

The next day they win the championship atop waves as high as telephone wires. I'm still ashamed, yet I can't help but smirk in deference to the dumb luck of the States. And I'll admit that I wanted to speak to an American by this time, albeit a sober, less slovenly type than the surfers before me. Perhaps this longing was what led me to Matthias.

I first saw him on the beach near the coconut men. He was looking out to sea, his belongings slumped beside him in a large duffle bag made of pieces of old blue jeans stitched together. A large stereo box played M's "Pop Musik" in the sand where he sat. His hair was wavy, blond, natural, not yet bleached straw by the sun, and he had on a pair of Ray-Bans sunglasses. I watched him half-smile as a pair of two-bit dope dealers hustled him. I laughed, glad that I'd soon be speaking of home, or if not home, a place bred in me, that I still remembered.

"Hey, you setting up camp?" I taunted.

"I look for place to stay." He spoke with a German accent.

Oh well, close enough. "You can share mine," I said. We rode off precariously on my bike; and when I rounded a turn, the load sent us crashing to the ground.

I stood up to a crowd of worried islanders, a chain of knitted eyebrows encircled us. Blood streamed down my leg, but it was only a bad scrape. Matthias seemed to be okay, so he got back on, but when I turned to join him on the bike, the crowd was in an uproar.

"Girl, you weigh down like Joe Heath mare." I assured them we'd be okay, that I'd be careful, but finally agreed to ride alone. Matthias would have to walk. I gave him directions to my hut and sped off.

I set up a bed in a corner of my hut. I didn't worry about the close quarters; I sensed no hint of sexual interest from Matthias, and knew now not to take this as any shortcoming on my part, but as the gift of a brother. Besides, with some health had come insomnia, filling my nights with the atonal atrophy of sleepless sighs. It'll be nice to have someone nearby. To listen to the lullaby of another's breath. I can't yet offer Peter, or anyone, my bed, but a far corner share with Matthias suits me.

I sit and smoke a Silk Cut the Papaya Queen has given me in turn for watching her "grandson," a six-year-old boy who spent the afternoon digging a hole with the dogs. By the time I finish the cigarette, the dogs are in a frenzy; they absolutely will not let anyone unintroduced by. The dogs and I have to have a meeting. I tell them that a brother has arrived and, begrudgingly, they let Matthias pass. Woof's tongue lolls and he stares dumbly. In the weeks to come they let him pass in silence if I'm present; only Woof continues to menace him physically, but with each advance he is instantly terrified with a low growl from Matthias.

Matthias and I speak of the world we inherited. He tells me about a place where order destroyed. Schoolchildren, from the West, were separated and grouped into sections deemed correct for their skills—none stayed together longer than four years. The Wall divided, and still Germany splintered itself into separate factions. Isolation is nothing if not productive.

Matthias evaded his country's service requirement. He knows that he'll have to return, but for now he wants to hear his thoughts, unfettered. "Vill be vorth das extra time ich dien," he says. That night, in talk before sleep, he apologizes for any noise; he warns me that he has dreams which turn to underwater screams, and that, although these screams are soundless within the dreams, they travel to the other side with a deafening fury. But his sleep, to me, remains silent.

In the nights to come, Matthias and I tool around town; we drink too much and create near-accidents on the Spring Garden Highway. Matthias revives in me an interest in Grasses, both Günter and that old helpmate pot—a potent combination. We laugh when the bartender who turns him on tells us why the Jaggers moved away: Jerry had been jailed, just one night, for picking up a crate of her own pot at the airport. "Mick en she leave fas' fas.' "

I don't mention Delia, but imagine her little snub nose snort at such silliness.

"Jerry must think she's on Saint Barts," said Matthias.

"Mm, maybe not tink at all."

I bask in their chat, but no matter how much I enjoy Matthias's companionship, I still need solitude. Only unattached can I coalesce.

I'm drawn more and more to the "bad" part of town that opens after two A.M., less to the clubs of Bridgetown, where the past surfaces and Matthias bums drinks from tourists of similar lineage. Something pulls me down—a craving for the underneath. Flashes of Crash blind me. I want to forego light and dwell beneath the canopy of stars, dim enough for my dilation; each bolt of wellness fills me with days, makes me fat from a future. So I wobble down to the crossroads where transvestites crack bottles on blacktop, and fight duels over lovers. (People without guns can be violently creative.) Fragments glisten on these streets like May Day confetti, like the aftermath of rain. Here, barefoot warriors tramp unscathed, and untouchables wander, discussing Grenada and Gilgamesh—I follow behind in tank top and torn military trousers, compelled by their fire.

"Don't go to the mountain," islanders tell me—that's what they call it, "the mountain." It's really no more than an alley atop landfill, but it's always been a pinnacle of the unknown. "Best you stay 'way—dem not real woman. Two spirits make dem wile."

The unwell are freed of desire, but if I'm to live, I, too, want to be wild. My old life is gone, and with it, the girl

I'd known. I don't have time to start from scratch with Woman 101—I need a crash course. Femininity is an art to the girls, a religion that they practice with a compulsory attentiveness; their "wild"-ness is the resultant fervor of devotees. I thought they could show me what Marcia might not—the externalization of what is felt within, executed by pros.

They would not have grabbed at Peter's pants.

Matthias insisted on coming with me once, but he is disturbed by the smashing of glass.

&

By one A.M., the lamplights are snuffed; the streets savage and serene. I drive slowly, helmetless. The air is all nitrate and charcoal, wind and crickets.

I park just outside of Bridgetown and walk the rest of the way to the wild side of the tracks, to knife fights and blood feuds, glitter and glam. I walk the narrow passageways between government buildings and citizens' shacks. I walk past bread crusts, Coke cans, spent typewriter ribbons and condoms. I keep walking until I emerge inside an alley citadel made from the turned backs of these buildings. I head straight for the bright light of a grill stand. The nine-fingered woman who mans the stand has been burned often. She doesn't smile; she doesn't skimp. I pay her two dollars and she hands me a liver cutter. "Cutter" means *sandwich*. "Bread baked in the dark rises highest," she says. I have a hero roll full of "blood food." Build red to outnumber the white, and set mast cells to sail. Still, white rises in me like stomachs emptied in a storm. It sur-

faces in silver and gray alongside the sienna of my sun-
burnt hair. This incongruous frame for so unwizened a face
makes me look not worldly, I think, but foolish.

Bones, like blood, can betray. The girls are mostly transvestites; few Bajans have the money for hormone therapy.
Besides, it can't change a jutting jaw, or size twelve pump.
The girls are so beautiful, though, that these features seem
endearing exoticisms.

I cringe to think that these goddesses are misfits, beaten
senseless by the light of day. I study their posture, and try
not to slump. Their necks are like regents', dissimilar only
in the manner of marks—instead of syphilis sores they
have scared scratches from their johns, covered not by ruf-
fles, but with airy swathes of silk, or by nothing at all. They
cross their legs at the ankle to smooth worn skirts, whose
need of mending remains obscured until dawn. And by
then there'll be more tears to sew. I watch this cycle—
concealment, then chaos.

I keep a certain distance, like a pigeon begging bread.
They grow used to me. I'd worried that I might unnerve
the girls, put them ill at ease, until I realize that, here,
there's little need for explanations. I sit, watch, and eat.
The tallest shoots me a wink on occasion; I, in turn, blush.
When I feel the color in my cheeks, I'm grateful that, like
the girls' five o'clock (A.M., that is) shadows, it can't be
detected in the dark.

At first, I call the girls "The Shadows," after Rodin's
sculpture, but then I see they are not like that at all. Now
I have names for them, but they're not their own names.
I call one Farm Girl, because of her choice of pet (live-
stock), and her resemblance to Ava Gardner. Farm Girl and
the tallest, who I've named Gloria for her great halo of

wool, often debate heatedly. Tonight's discussion seems to be on the nature of truth. They pause to argue as they tweeze each other's eyebrows by the rigged single bulb, soaking power from the courthouse.

"You a li-ah," says Farm Girl.

"Why call so?" asks Gloria.

"Cause what's real ain't what's true."

"You real ugly," says Gloria.

"Dat ain't true."

"Is too. And dat politician you screw, he married."

"Ain't true. He love me real an true," says Farm Girl.

"He love he real woman," says Gloria.

"I true woman," says Farm Girl, and grabs Gloria's nose with the tweezers.

"You ugly he-she." Gloria says this in my direction, like waste spouting from a gutter on an unknown passerby. Gloria stands her ground.

But Farm Girl persists. Until Gloria kicks Farm Girl, grabs the tweezers, pulls out a switchblade, and then lunges at the pet.

"Stop now—or I slit dis animal like a Muslim at holiday. Damn goat."

"She a *sheep!*" says Farm Girl.

"Goat—"

"Sheep—"

"Goat."

"Liiii—uh," yells Farm Girl. The black-bellied sheep, genus unknown (it looks more like a goat), has all this time sat quietly beside Farm Girl like a contented dog. Now he/ she sheep/goat lets out a resounding bleat, and bolts. The third girl, whom I call Polly, because she's pretty, runs after sheep-goat.

"You rasso girl-chiles, actin' like you ain grown 'tall," she says. She makes the same sound of disgust that I do when something interrupts my reading, a grunt like a cat unfed. I wave my sandwich at sheep-goat.

"Ba-aah, ba-aah," I say, a bit sheepishly. Sheep-goat turns to me like a union boss to a republican. I step back in a half-bow and again wave the sandwich. Sheep-goat snatches it up and chews, still suspicious in its half-cocked dog look. The trio preens a bit, then comes over to present themselves. This is when I learn their names. Ava is Thalia, Gloria is Clio—and pretty *is* Polly.

"Tanks a bunch," says Thalia, scratching the contented animal behind its ears. Up close, Polly sees the marks on my exposed arms.

"Johnnie do dat to you?" she asks.

"No," I say. The paisley is no longer raised. Flat, it lacks the dimension of illness.

"You do dat to you?" Clio asks.

"I don't think so." I feel freedom when I say this. Clio's practice of self-mutilation is visible up close—the cross-hatched razorings inside her forearms resemble tiny tic-tac-toe games. She stands behind me tracing the patterns below my shoulder in a tickle—Queen Bee; I think she must be pollinating me. "Beauty, beauty," she says, "c'mon out."

"Beauty opens doors like a thief," I say.

"Betta ta steal den beg."

I shrink beneath my veil of half-matted hair. Polly pulls the shock from my eyes and pins it with something lifted from her own satin mane, then she takes out the kohl she uses on her red-rimmed eyes. I shut my lids, expecting the same, but instead she draws gently atop the scrolls of my forearm. "Dat's what I'd do, if I was you; mon o'mon, dey'd call me Python Polly, betcha I get mo date, yeah mon!" she urges.

"But I thought *symmetry* was beauty," I say.

"Oh no," Polly says, "dat jus' for doz dat can't focus."

Thalia wipes my neck with a damp washcloth. "Wassa madder?" she says and shakes her head. "You hatch in da mud, dirty girl?"

I'd made peace with my paisley, but still see it as unsightly. And the scars that set the girls apart seem to me not offensive but sad. Yet I think the girls themselves beautiful, and wish to be like them. To highlight, not hide. But I cannot believe in their exaltation of scars.

I insist on wearing my Converses, seared soles and all, while the girls tango barefoot upon the sparkling street. I've lost the courage. When they ask me to join the dance, I protest. "I'm just a visitor," I say, "on my way out."

"Girl," says Clio, "you ain' goin' nowhere."

The girls school me in surfaces. I follow their instruction and layer my lips with pencil and rouge and pencil again. "Porno lips," says Polly, "won't eat off no matter what, no matter how many times." I think of lip gloss and lesser times, and draw a line of imperceptible black to enhance my eyes. Thalia, who is a Trini of East Indian descent, teaches me (or tries) to maneuver a thread so that it will remove a thatch of body hair.

"Oh man," I say, "*this* is stratagem for the enemy."

"Beauty is pain," she says.

"Oh, I thought that was just French for bread."

"Okay, rasso girl," says Thalia, "time for da hair we keep."

I curl a strand around my index finger and wait as instructed; the girls tease their locks higher, but I don't expect mine to take in the damp. I shiver and realize the cold is from dew. The cast of unrisen sun behind the girls makes burning bush of their henna-soaked hair. On my bike ride home, I pray for two spirits of my own—one to die and one to live.

I'm greeted at the gates by the somnolent scoldings of dogs, frustrated they can no longer keep me in. I reach down to gather their noses, sneezing for attention, into my lap. The blue is beginning and I direct my entourage to the concrete beside my bed, then I mouth "sweet dreams" to an already sleeping Matthias. I notice that chest down, he is a thin ambiguous form, his body curved lightly and nearly hairless. I wonder if he's lucky enough to have two spirits, then I'm asleep.

That night I dream the sea parts, allowing me to enter its depths, but once below, unwieldy with flesh, I bob to the surface. When I awake, I crush the pillow to my face and throw it across the room in frustration when my body, independent of me, won't smother.

I know then that if I live, Life will be less surmountable than Death.

I sit on the shore and look at the Christ Church villa. It's empty now. It appears to have gone empty for some time. Bougainvillea climbs uncut in a mania of greenery, its leaves spotted like the gums of beggars. Topiary has turned into something that blocks the sun, and just as I rise to leave, a shadow is cast over me. The size of it suggests the past. And in a moment of prophecy—the kind whose validity one always questions—I know whose it is and, expecting myself wrong, turn toward him.

Monarch had caught up at the beach with Delia and me later that long-ago summer and offered us each a thousand dollars to "escort" his friends. We tried to pass by him, but he persisted. "My friends come often, but not too— you could make $100,000 if you stayed here. Believe me," he'd said. Time froze for a moment while we'd considered this easy way out of our domestic indenture—then I'd laughed at him, but Delia began to cry.

"He thinks we're prostitutes," she said.

I never could decide whether her reaction, or my own, bothered me more.

Monarch is more immense than I'd remembered—Goliath with Birkenstocks and a Harvard education. He wears the latter discreetly, like a weapon unattainable to others, but it designates him a despot. In the past, the false security of an apparently gilded life, along with a buffer of tourism, had been between us, so I was able to see him as a mirage, and thus slip away from specifics, that remained, to me, unknown, but still unsavory. Now I'm an inhabitant of his world—made an inside-out Cinderella by an increment of change. His shadow draws the light from me. I take my prescription Vuarnets off, to ensure that he's indeed the same man, but without the lenses I see as I always have in dreams, indefinite and in dusk.

I rise, move closer, squint to see, but the sun catches my eye.

"My friend, are you all right?" he asks. Though I'm covered by a caftan, he sees still that I've been ill.

"Yes, it must be the heat," I answer. He reaches for me; I flinch.

"I know you," he says. I have no reply. He takes my silence as vacancy, and tries to move in.

"Do you remember me? You must," he says. I say nothing, but dwell on the seam of his memory. Like any scar, I can't help but toy with it.

He extends his hand. "I won't hurt you," he says, "believe me."

Still I sense harm. Smell it in the fear that ferries through the day's dank vapor, alighting like a botfly to linger under skin, until my own weakness brings it to fruition. I don't know what he wants this time, only that it's foul, like a dead thing brought to half-life by dread. At least my devalued body is safe, secured finally by its wilt. Or is there a market for my kind? A discount for day-old flowers.

"You live here now?" he says. I shrug. "How can you stand such a lack of erudition? I myself loathe it."

"Then why didn't you stay in Cambridge?" I ask. He's silent now.

"No one believes in me there."

"Walk with me," he says. We walk a half mile or so. He points to a bevy of statuesque blondes and I see them lounging like bored panthers. "Mine," he says, "I have more Germans than Americans. And these are not so bright; that is why you interest me. You're smart. I can offer such a smart girl the world and all its currency."

"I don't feel smart." I don't explain the extent of my ignorance—that I've been emptied of all I'd known. And I can't figure out why he values intelligence so highly in a call girl. Then I realize, *of course*, he wants to expand the income of his empire using the tricks of his sisters. I'd learned of these tricks through afternoons of island gossip with the Papaya Queen.

"Dey get dem wid da drink, an den dey tief em." The Queen clucked her tongue while I signaled admiration with a high five; before she met it, she looked around to see if she was being observed in such foolishness. "Every bush a man," she explained, then told me how the island girls roll rich tourist men: They steal their wallets after the men pass out from drink that's either too strong with alcohol, or helped along by a kick of something more. I couldn't help but applaud—I consider it more a check (or debit) on hypocrisy than an actual robbery. I know that the

139

men, British mostly, never behave this way in their own country. Here they cavort, in all manners of exposure, sometimes behind bushes, others before children not their own; they defame the legacy of propriety that they, themselves, had imposed upon the islanders—who, in turn, change repression into dignity. They keep their shirts on in the grocery store, but lay themselves bare before lovers. In the North true nakedness is furtive, though the disrobed are pervasive in posters, like stains that cling stubbornly to the sides of buildings and buses. I can't fault the girls for feeding their children with the lucre of lechers—in fact, I support them.

I expect Monarch desires dominion. But if he tricks the tricks, the clients won't come back. The stable will be short-lived. "What, exactly, do you want from me?" I ask.

"To pick up a few of my favorite things, as I do not wish to leave the country."

All at once I know that he can't leave—there is little, if anything, he can do on his own.

He only wants me to be his mule. Of course. My body's built for burden now, not pleasure. I try to appear impassive before a man who'd love to laugh at such folly. Then, upping him, I laugh myself—that the blight of vanity could still cling to a skin so slick with paisley *is* amusing.

"Don't they fetch?" I motion toward the panthers, ever blonder.

"Sometimes," he smirks elongating the yes to a hiss, "but only a few can bring it back to me."

"Which ones?"

"They're not present," he says. I don't press for their

whereabouts; I don't want his lies; it's possible I'm already thick in hookah smoke, here, in this other Christ Church.

"How much do they make?" I ask.

"More than you need," he says.

This time he tells me the truth.

~

I care less for myself than I have in a while.

I lose sleep, then taste. When the girls see me pass nights with no cutter, I smell their disappointment like bread burning, like a thing forgotten remembered too late. When I ask them for a tincture to cover scars, it's as if I've begged hemlock. Again, I grow ill. At this juncture, it's a snap. White like larvae slips stillborn from unhealed scrapes. I leave lessons learned like things forgotten, to rot. And remember only that paisley goes with nothing.

My whirls, the walls, again, comprise my world. I am unable to sit stationary, but cannot move forward. The sweet life inspissates me. Now that a foot, grounded, is out of the grave, nothing fits.

I slip it back in—it feels sublime.

I subsist on air; I need nothing more. I refuse the overcooked noodles Matthias offers, and pretend to be asleep when he tries to speak to me. When the Papaya Queen comes to call, I say, "I don't want company." Matthias leaves me alone, more out of anger than from consideration, his skin grows dark from sleeping on sand, under sun, away from me and my four white walls. My own skin becomes chalky—except for my paisley, etched like the seismic scrawl of a mad child. My lips crack and swell. I see things scutter that are not there. I believe that I'm weeding myself, crooked twig unbud, from the earth.

The army of days retreats until I am left alone, unburdened. Futureless.

When I run out of cigarettes and rum, Matthias refuses to get more. He lies reading Rilke. Thin-hipped rump up. I raise a lid and say, "On earth, I'm the panther," but he sneers, and continues to eat his overcooked noodles (I call them the Anti-*dente*).

" 'There is no place that does not see you,' " he says clearly. " 'You must change your life.' " God, I think, this from a sibling so insubstantial that he appeared to me washed up on shore.

"I'm not hiding," I say, "besides, soon there'll be nothing left to see—for anyone to stare at."

"Wrong," he says, "I'll see you in my dreams, your *nothing* will be my screams," then adds an afterthought, like a bit of salt, "Ass-wipe."

"Who taught you that—or did you just make it up?" I ask.

"I forget—ass-wipe," he says and tosses the book over-bed, then singsongs an aside, to whom, I'm not sure, "*Labour, and sorrow, and learn, and forget . . .*"

"That's not Rilke," I say. He shakes his head, then smothers it in a pillow, as if to protect himself from an oncoming uproar.

The dogs are barking again. Their howls have grown louder since my self-confinement. They sit pointedly by the gates, allowing no one past. I wonder who or what they bark at. Has Peter Rock come by? Or is it just phantoms?

I have no way of knowing, no phone, no letterbox; Matthias is my only messenger, and he's not pleased with me. Still, he's been enjoying unlimited use of the bike, that must count for something. He's here tonight with me; I'm glad he's not outside on the sand. I hear him yawn and follow his lead to sleep, to dream. It comes easier now.

There is dark, there is light, there is paisley. I watch as Rilke smashes these symbols, "like ice for the martinis we'll have when man moves forward," he tells me.

I wake up within my dreams in an obscurity, unescorted. I'm so thirsty that I wonder what it would feel like to drink light. But even the shades are shut tight. I scratch at them like a cat. Not a bird. Not a ray. Only darkness, and silence. The silence of abandonment—the silence of a ghost town. Nothing tangible but thirst.

I'm tired, and feel for something to lie down on, but can touch nothing. Suddenly I'm afraid. That's when Death comes to me looking like Anthony Quinn, and says, in annoyance, "I divorced you long ago."

I awake just as I'm finding my way. Still parched, I gulp and grab—a glass of water, plate of noodles (firm), and a note from Matthias.

> *Hey You—Panther Girl (Ha)*
> *Gone out for Cigarettes*
> *Wish You Were*
>
> *—M*

No map, but there is my exposed skin. And upon it the circuitous path I've been following. I ascend to descend, then back again. A squiggle of starts and stops, scrawled in blood. Why do such omniscient cells breed forgetfulness? Perhaps because the past is mostly myth.

Still blind, I change my mind. Again. It's a woman's prerogative. The dream that may come has given me pause. But how to live? And with what?

∾

There is much dough to be gotten by those who roll in the flour— just be careful you don't get baked. I'd overheard Ralph the roadie say this, just before he again offered me his wares free, and Crash fired him. But Crash has dashed—and I'm doughless.

"Yes," I say.

Monarch looks up from the *Wall Street Journal,* yesterday's edition. "That's my girl."

He gives me an itinerary, he pays cash.

I pay credence, squeeze the spectrum of dollars, Trini, Bajan, and U.S., tight in palms that itch like an illness.

I feel like I'm dying.

∾

The taxi winds through the streets toward the airport, and I stare out unfocused, unraveling reasons like spools in my mother's sewing tin (she always hid silk under cotton). But no matter what reason I come up with, it's always inextricably tangled to one thread—the avoidance of asking anything of anyone. It all came down to this one backhanded "fuck you." I'd forgone suicide, the mother of them all. My fuck-yous were getting smaller, but they marched like

144

Seuss characters crazy toward that corner conclusion—that the *you* in fuck, is me.

Outside the sky interjects rain, an achromatized gray to get lost in. The sun is setting, and from the backseat I, in my white Lone Ranger boots with room enough for half a kilo—my only footwear that, subtly spotted, remained unrotted—ride off into its gunmetal drop.

I'll admit that the boots are a prop. The Monarch had explained to me (between bites of bialy and pages of greed) how cocaine is pressed between microthin plastic, so that if I'm frisked by authorities, they'll (seem to) feel only flesh. There are, as of yet, no dogs in Caribbean airports. No beasts to nose my ice-swaddled sweat, and catch me cold. And so, wrapped fish fashion, in fetish sheets, I, devolved, will cross borders.

The driver pulls into the airport and tries to overcharge me. "You think I'm some naive tourist?" I quote the standard fare, and curse at him in Bajan. But his perception has eased my mind, so I leave the difference as a tip. It's late. I rush through the empty cavern of Grantley Adams International, past the red leaf of Air Canada—past the Pan Am globe spinning its innumerable blue lines, like unsprung veins. I run past them all until, breathless, I arrive at BWIA.

"The eight o'clock to Trinidad." I reach in my pockets to pluck reds and blues like plumage from my carrion. I hoard green, careful not to spend it yet.

"Return ticket to port of origin please," the attendant says.

"Oh—what's that?"

"Your ticket home—to da States perhaps?"

"Oh," I say. The fluorescents buzz a warning, emblazon a bruise on the palm that holds my passport. When I see that her wound is just ink, it's no less an omen.

"You vex, girl?"

"Yes," I say, with certainty.

"The ticket . . ."

"I don't have it."

"Do you know where you're going?" she asks. The answer eludes me—it's never been etched in my mind with adrenaline importance. "If you don't know where you're going, it's helpful to know where you're from," the woman says. I say nothing. "Where? Where are you from? You need a ticket back!" The woman pounds me with epitaph, like a mad mason at an unmarked grave. "Canada?" she asks hopefully.

"The States," I say. But it's the wrong answer. She refuses to sell me a ticket to Trinidad.

"You can't get dere from here, until I see dat you can get home."

"I have no home," I say.

"Ha! I knew it. But you don't look like no hippie."

"What? I'm too young to be a hippie—and what do you have against hippies anyhow?"

"Dey love beaches."

"So?"

"So dey sleep on sand, an make der home on beaches dat ain' ders. You need a ticket back. Dat's da rule."

Finally we reach a compromise: She'll let me out but they won't let me back in until Matthias shows them my return ticket to the States. I call a pay phone near the Papaya

Queen. It rings, and rings, but just as I'm about to hang up, a stranger answers.

"Who's this?" I ask.

"King Domino," the voice says.

"Um, King, do you know the Papaya Queen?" I'm soothed by the background sounds of rhythmic clacks and laughter.

"Sure do."

"And do you know her grandson?"

"That boy ain't her grandson."

"But you know him?"

"Sure do."

"Um, could you please tell him to tell Matthias to bring the Eastern ticket to New York behind the picture of David Hasselhoff to Gate Eight at the airport on Wednesday at 7:30 A.M.?" All our valuables are behind Hasselhoff.

"Sure could," King says.

"Sure?"

"Sure," he says, as if I'd insulted him.

I thank him, and apologize for my intrusion on his game.

"Do you remember where you're going?" the attendant asks.

"Trinidad," I say and she sells me a ticket.

"You're leaving Barbados," she warns, inferring that if my friend doesn't come through, I'll be in limbo. I think of a pale blue in-between, a fate more benevolent than she wants me to imagine.

Two stout men stand behind a red velvet rope before the BWIA gate. I think of how size gives them the illusion of strength. I show them my ticket and passport.

"Return ticket to point of embarkment?" asks the elder.

147

"I left it at home." I think of Woof and his simple question face, and will an ignorant veil across my eyes.

"Why Trinidad?" they ask in unison. *Why indeed*. The answer jangles around my mind like forgotten change in the lining of a coat, impossible to get to.

"To drill for oil." I can't help but laugh. The men assume I'm flirting with them. And they believe me. It must be the boots.

"You a leetel late, lady. Trini, she stripped bare ass as baby boy, an dry as old woman."

"Oh," I say.

"But Tobago is nice now," says the elder, "jus don go on de weekend—den she full of shithead Sunoco men."

The younger hands me my bag. "I'm Percival," he says, then bends close to my ear, and whispers, "I work Sunday, so I'll meet your plane that morning, 7:10 sharp." They lift the velvet rope, let me pass.

I wait by the gate. When the call comes to board, I walk the gangplank pale and damp, excreting the dour odor of a liar—all sulphur and remorse.

༄

Inside the cabin, I wade among the waves of others. The scent of coconuts and sweat hits me like a breaker and I'm swept up in a salt sea of departure. I blast the Grateful Dead, "Box of Rain," on my battered leaking lemon walkman and wonder who chose such a cowardly color. I sit rigid with apprehension, silent with secrets. Only my heart belies me, yammering into the night as we continue to climb. A change in pressure could alter the precarious composition of my body—the possibilities of decline are endless. I chew gum to protect what I can, my ears from an insignificant pain. The temperature rises, the pressure increases, and I can't help but think that, like a life raft sprung too soon, I'll burst. I panic and pop ten Seldane. My ears ring. But nothing happens.

The lights of Port-of-Spain break through the black like pinpricks in a widow's crepe. They blink and gawk while I, a bird of prey, circle. Perhaps the illuminated shacks are signaling, granting me the momentary revelation that, although they're victims, they're not benign. Without warning, delousing disinfectant is sprayed. I spit into a napkin and wait for my breathing to stop. It doesn't. I pull down the long sleeves of my "World Cup" surfer t-shirt, and, secure that my paisley is obscured, I deplane.

At customs, the young couple before me begins to quarrel. The man is South American—his accent lies between lisped European and strapping Mexican, but I can't pin it down. The girl is mostly silent, maybe Canadian. Her sapphire eyes, wide with alarm, give her the look of a sunbasked Alice locked beyond a broken glass. The ginger-haired infant seated on her hip coos in spite of his caretakers' quibbling. *She's too young. Younger than me.* I'd never had such thoughts before, and realize in horror that I envy a mother her baby boy.

Alice's man is shorter but certainly not slighter than her. When they reach the immigration booth, the newlyweds, as I think of them, are banished to the guarded room just before the exit. The steel door to the room is conspicuous among so much wood. Alice stands inert—until her man calls, "Ale—ssandra! Alesandra!" She turns slowly toward him, the guards, the metal door. "I hate this shit," he says as she approaches. Alesandra tries to give her baby to one of the guards. He refuses, and ushers the family in.

I wonder what "shit" he referred to. Wonder at how close my name for her was to her own name, about what constitutes reality. And how much cocaine can fit in a child's diaper. I wonder why I'm here. I stare at the newlyweds as they recede, and half-believe that if I concentrate, my gaze will prevent their fate. I fix my hopes upon them, and watch as the door slams shut. Half-belief and hope are as useless a preservation as smashed glass.

It's my turn now. "You don't have your return ticket," the immigration officer says in disbelief. "You can't possibly be admitted."

"Then send me back." I'm relieved. He curls one side of his mouth and chews his mustache. I think of ourobouros, but he remains.

"But you haven't arrived. Why go back?"

"Fear?" I say.

"Of what?"

"Mosquitoes," I say and pull up my sleeves.

"Jesus, I've never seen bites like that," he says. "Well, you won't be getting any here unless you have a ticket home."

"I don't have my ticket with me. It's back at my hotel in Barbados." I think of my "hotel" and if King, the roadside concierge, has caught up with Matthias yet.

The officer eyes the clock; it's near closing time (the next flight in isn't due until morning). He feigns boredom, yawns, and says, "Well, I'll have to take your word for it."

"On my honor." A spooked shiver ripples my spine into

a hook, as if to sweep my bottom for truths. I stay there bent like a vulture over the paperwork to avoid his gaze. The man stamps my passport, and waves me by. The strictest regulations in the Caribbean were bent in a matter of minutes. South America is less than seven miles away, and people are held in jail for far lesser violations than mine. I knew this before the newlyweds were banished. The man never asked me why, where, or how.

And I no longer knew any of it.

∽

My cab driver downs coffee all the way to the Happy Holiday Lodge. He introduces himself as Amariit Singh, but says I can call him Jitters. When he asks my name, I look toward a distant Sunoco sign. "Sunny," I say, though I feel distinctly un-. Jitters is paternal, and proud of his country. His "new India," he calls it.

"I am relieved that I did not have to abandon my heritage," he says, then looks into the rearview mirror and asks, "What is American heritage?"

"Just a magazine," I tell him. He falls silent with incomprehension and turns down an unlit road. We drive beneath towering groves of grape- and breadfruit trees. Their green ceiling keeps out the stars. And perhaps, too, the downward gaze of the North.

I notice that the foliage is denser here than on the rock of Barbados; in an instant one could lose her way, but, with Jitters at the helm, I feel safe. He explains each sight. There are ten-story buildings next to shacks. There are Gothic cathedrals, Hindu temples, and Moslem mosques.

Jitters tells me of a mountain, invisible in the dark, that recently suffered a brushfire. "The bamboo exploded, and everything went black."

"I'm sorry," I say.

"No need. Nature, she on our side here. A few showers and the mountain she green as good money." I stare out into the countryside, enthralled, while beneath us cobble becomes stone becomes gravel and so on until tar. The change in surface brings dimension to our winding trajectory; this, coupled with the heady air, makes me nauseous. Then suddenly, like a mother's hand massaging a sick child, comes the scent of eucalyptus. Soothed and anointed, I drift off to sleep.

I'm jerked by the centrifugal pull of a roundabout toward a chrome pillar thrust up high from the earth. I survey the surface of the hotel and see that there are no edges to cling to if one should fall. I place too many gray-green bills into the driver's hand, as if pre-purchasing penance. It's the first time this trip that I've relinquished U.S. currency. I stand motionless, close to Jitters. I'm reluctant to leave this moment for my next. "Goodnight. Maybe I'll see you again," he says.

"That'd be nice." I savor his breath, all curry and coffee.

There are no doormen, so I tug with all my strength at the brass-handled entrance, until I'm met by a frozen gash of fragrantless air. *What scent might emerge if the power was cut?* The lobby is empty. There's no vestibule to prepare one for this lonely pastel palace. The only person in view is a red-vested man polishing goblets at the bar. The serenade that emanates from its poor quality speakers tinkles as if it's being played on his glassware. I listen closer and discover that these sounds are the strains of Crash's last hit single set to Muzak. My mind must be playing tricks, I think, but when I turn to confront my musical mirage, it falls silent.

I look toward the mini-replica of Niagara Falls in the center of the lobby—and it stops. There was one like this at my cousin's wedding reception. Another man, in another red vest, turned it off whenever someone made a toast. It's plastic. Another petroleum product extruded into being while sculptors strain a lifetime for motion in bronze. I drag my vinyl suitcase to reception, and ask for a room. The attendant moves like a ghost, then yawns as if it's taking all her energy just to appear there before me. "We have no rooms left, only suites," she says.

"But I had a reservatiòn."

"It says here it's been canceled."

"*What?* Says who?" I say.

"Says the machine."

"So how much is the upgrade gonna set me back?"

"A lot," she says. I give her my credit card, even though I can be traced with it; I don't want to give up any more cash.

"I'm sorry, but we're full," she says after touching a few keys, then mumbles something that sounds to me like "weightless."

"What?" I ask.

"I'll waitlist you."

"But you said you had suites."

"They're reserved . . . oh wait, here we are," she says and gives me an oversized key. "You're lucky. We're *almost* full."

"Almost," I say, and feel this luck like the proverbial bird shit.

I fling open the door and throw my suitcase on the bed, but before I have a chance to wash up, throw up, or turn on the television, the phone rings. I answer. "Singh here. I'm coming up." The voice is abrasive, *definitely* not Jitters's.

"Fine," I say this as a dare, then realize I'm asserting myself to a dial tone.

I scan the walls for those famous hotel peepholes, but find nothing in the colonial wallpaper, just a clock that proclaims an hour much later than expected. The passage of time stuns me, and before I've recovered, there comes a knock at the door.

"Who is it?" I say. I hope for a mint-bearing chambermaid, but look through the keyhole and see, instead, a wolf. A man, actually, but his face is that of a wolf. His eyes are fires. His nose flares from his face like a blunt instrument, and flecks of white, big as bone bits, speckle his shaggy unwashed hair. He is repulsive, arresting.

"Open up," he says, and knocks again.

"Who is it?" I repeat.

"Singh," he says, then turns, as if aware of my gaze, and begins to pick his teeth. Bone bits, perhaps. He uses one unclipped claw, the rest are kept short. I crack the door; he forces it open, and strides in. He smells like meat and malice. I retreat and open a window.

"Where da bathroom?" he asks. *Yikes.* I point haphazardly toward the hall, as if perhaps he might get lost without adequate instruction. The door slams shut and, mercifully, I hear the hum of an exhaust system. But no tap, no flush. He emerges, eyes ablaze, brow beaded with sweat. He chatters incessantly on the quality of Holiday End's toilet paper. "Nice for da bum," he says, and stares at mine. He's stoned—on his own product, by the looks of it. I don't stop to ponder the implications of this. I just want him out of my suite.

"Okay, let's get down to business," I say.

He sprawls on a flowered bed—I make a mental note to sleep on the other.

"Business," I repeat.

He pats the bed, inviting me to "conference."

I move away, point to the pattern on the spread. "There aren't any dogwoods in the Caribbean, are there?"

"I abhor horticulture," says Singh.

"Why?" I ask. But he's ceased to listen. He's busy perusing room service, and I can see from his bulging pockets that he's swiped the hotel soap and shampoo.

"This food is very expensive." He continues to pick his teeth. "I'm hungry."

How can he be hungry?! He probably sleeps on the stuff, too. I'm horrified, and a little in awe. The thought of him lingering here to masticate, or sleep, on my bed, impels me to action. I think quick and lie. "I'm hungry too, but I want something indigenous, not from room service."

"Yes," he agrees, and belches, "I also want something to digest."

The warning signs are there, yet I ignore them, like a headstrong child at a thin ice pond. Drug lords are a rich lot—it seems odd that a room service menu, one from the Happy Holiday Lodge, not the Ritz, could invoke such assessment. Were drug lords now on a budget? Wasn't easy cash and excess their raison d'être? Was Wolf's consumption of product wise? (It was a no-no in the movies.) I gloss over these glitches with more brevity than wisdom. I reason he's just cheap—and life's not like the movies.

"Let's go," he says.

"A roti would be nice," I say, half-believing it. A roti is potatoes, spice, and maybe more, rolled in flatbread.

Peter had warned me that, in Trinidad, rotis could be dangerous. A week ago, a world away, I'd gone to his place to fetch my bike from a tune-up. But when I arrived, I found he hadn't yet touched it. I couldn't decide whether this was a way to keep me around, immobile—or whether I and my concerns were no longer his priority.

While he worked, I drank the last of his guava juice, and harangued him about the Bajan bus system. I'd shared the bus ride over with a delegation of island chickens, who surrounded me, all disapproving mothers, and snatched away my mustard sandwich as if it was tooth-rotting candy. (The Papaya Queen was sad that day because she had no fillings, but she still charged me for the sandwich.) I kvetched about all this to Peter, but I didn't really care about the lunch, what bothered me was that Peter hadn't allowed me to borrow his bike. "It's too big for you," he insisted. I interpreted his concern for safety as a ploy to make me feel small—so I went for his soft spot. "Tell me about Trinidad," I asked.

"Not a ting to tell," he scowled. "Why you ask so? You goin dare or sumting?"

"Maybe, something," I said soft, afraid that he'd ask "whyfor." But he didn't.

"Go on den," he said. I couldn't tell whether he was angered by my interest in Trinidad, or the chance that I'd leave. Or because I drank the last of the guava. "But stay 'way from dose buses dare, don' ever get too close," he warned.

"Why?" I asked, thinking of toxic effluent.

"Cause you're sure to be hit."

"Drivers that bad, huh."

"No, not drivers. Passengers, dey hit you wid one of tree tings."

"And what would these three things be?"

"You'd like to know, huh?" He lowered his voice, spoke slow. And rested hands on my thighs.

"Yes, I'd like to know." I was at the mercy of his reply.

"First, you must promise me."

"What?"

"That you will never again bewitch my dogs." I scratched the one who looked searchingly at me. I wanted to ask what exactly the constraints were, but instead I gave in.

"Fine," I said, and kept scratching.

"Okay den—if you get near a Trini bus you are sure to be hit wid: a roti, a bible, or a bottle of rum."

"Yo ho ho."

"You like roti?" Wolf grins, and bares shards of snaggle-teeth.

"Yes, I do." I think of Peter, and of my own ignored intuitions. Then I rifle through my suitcase for the Papaya Queen's talisman, a six-inch blade she gave me when I'd stayed out so late that she took to calling me Early Girl. Wolf doesn't see me slip it inside my boot; he's chugging minibar bourbon and tripping through channels on the satellite tv.

We take the elevator to the garage. The beep that announces each floor sounds like a signal for detonation. Our descent seems to take forever, our time underneath longer. Finally, an attendant appears to lift the gate and let us loose on the world. We drive off in a Kia toward town.

Singh's motor shifts into too high a cruising speed, wails in protest, then sputters out. I grapple with this inertia by wriggling toes inside my Converses, a "sign of spirit possession," the Papaya Queen had warned.

"First we go for drink, cold Caribe." He pronounces it carob.

"Why for?" I say.

He just looks at me blankly.

I'm frustrated with myself for playing along, with him for trying to play me out; I want to complete a pick-up, not be one. His car, a tin box of immobility, with so much debris beneath my fidgeting feet, stalls—as if in punctuation to his monumental moment of intrusion. *Let's go for a drink*.

I could have killed him then. Like a skin-piercing insect.

But instead I say, "One drink." And turn my face out the window to hide its rage. I'm just as angry at myself. The mercy of this eludes me; when I look out, I see only my own face staring back in accusal. "Those cigarettes are vile," I say. "What kind do you smoke?" I like to discover brands and compare their offensiveness.

"Black cigarettes, you try one."

"No. No thanks." I know by the tone of his voice that they're rolled with drugs. "Black from hash?" I say. As ever, I'm interested in nomenclature, but the lure of language can be a downfall.

"Cocaine, from da way day burn," he says. He lights up, and I remember this was the same acrid scent that tinged concert halls. "The drug of assholes," Crash had called it. And heroin? "The drug of saints." I'd thought only the wicked sought such roles. Anyway, I was right—Singh partook of his own product.

"Is that the stuff I'm supposed to pick up?" I point to his smoke.

"No mon," he says, possessively, "it not here yet."

"What d'ya mean, 'It not here yet'? Is it back at the hotel?"

He shakes his head.

"Are we going to get it now?"

"No, we go for drink—cold Caribe."

"Fine. But where's the product?" That's what they called it in the movies.

He shrugs, and smokes furiously.

My eyes burn, my ears ring. I imagine an alarm is sounding, though I know it's just too much Seldane. I also know a professional is able to locate, but does *not* partake of, his product. No wonder the country is in the state it is, I think, then immediately rescind the notion, sickened by my bigotry, as always born of desperation. I know better—I know the U.S. demands, and that the South is no pusher. Trinidad, bereft of its oil but still seven miles de Sud America, is just a pick-up point for the North's needs. I feel nauseous.

Singh pulls into a hamburger stand and buys two beers. They drip with icy water from the cooler that serves as both refrigerator and bench. The cold feels good against my skin. The Caribe clears my mind, combs the tangle of thoughts.

I should not be here. The silence of cellophane uncrimped persists, then meaning surfaces: Monarch had decreed there'd be a chance I'd be called the first night, but that I wouldn't be contacted until two hours before my departure time. Time enough to be wrapped and stuffed, like a venom-laden present. I'd missed the implicit—calling was not contact. So why was I here?

I step out into the night unhinged. Motion to a rasta by the roadside, while Singh, by the stand, slurps goat grease.

The Papaya Queen had given me the knife, but only to place beneath my pillow, "to cut da pain, should it sneak back at night." My talisman had traveled, sock in suitcase, with me. Now, it itches to be removed from my boot. I need to calm down.

I pull out the second U.S. five of the evening, and approach the rasta. "I need what you have and it ain't your good looks."

"An who is da man, dat I may be made answer to?" He points to Singh. His look is a mixture of sorrow and indictment, and I know then that he thinks me a prostitute. I compose a lament in my head just then for the wolf and me, a dirge set to bongos, something that could not be Muzaked.

Why are you going?

I should not be here.

Who is the man?

He should not be.

"He's nobody." I'm surprised by the tone of my voice—it sounds like Monarch. I scratch inside my boot.

"Mosquito, dey bad tonight," the rasta says, then asks, "You ire?"

"I'll be better when I'm stoned—sell me your best."

"La-dee I no *sell* nothing, I ave enough problem here

jus' wearing my hair, but I give you my own spliff, an it da best, ta be sure." He waves the bill away.

I insist, dole gray-green gratuity to assuage my guilt. Then give him another.

Singh is back in the car; I can tell from the direction of his belches. He has neither roti nor greasy goat for me. I slide in, light up. And smoke. I feel less, I feel better.

"You should not talk to rasta," Singh says. I see the fear and disdain that one stranger can harbor for another. I sip my Caribe, and smoke some more, like an asthmatic victim at his inhaler, then ask,

"*Why* did you come up to my room tonight?"

He slouches and I see his light sweat well to droplets. "You have boyfriend? Where are you from? You have children? Where are your parents from?"

"I have nothing." I scratch madly at my ankle.

"There is the disease there, yes, but I will never catch it. My blood she is too strong," he says in an unconvincing bravado. *Why on earth this sudden non sequitur?* Has he noticed my affliction? Or are his foremost thoughts representative of the nation's? Does the country, conquered time and again for its resources, until its inhabitants, beaten back and capped with Texaco stars, now brace for an invasion of the body?

Bad blood drips from the north; the hemisphere is all a Twombly.

"Black cigarette?" Singh asks again.

"No. *No cocaine.*"

"Why? Are you scared to get high with me—scared of what you might do?" he says.

"Yes."

I fix on his jugular; this soothes me.

"I have plan to expand into Boston—on my own. I want to be your boyfriend, to snuggle up and sleep with you. To take care of you."

My toes clench uncontrollably. The hand inside my boot shakes with a terrible palsy. "I *don't want* that."

"But we be famous."

"Oh—that'd be good for business."

My blood-filled eyes are burnt by the smoke, his acrid offering to an idiot god. But this loss of faculties seems only to make my hearing more acute—and his tiny snort of discontent comes as a roar.

"Take me back, *now*," I demand. And he does.

When I return, I dial the number on the tiny slip of torn *Wall Street Journal*. Monarch had given it to me, along with the money. "Rikki don't lose that number," he'd said. They must play a lot of Steely Dan in Cambridge. The phone rings three times and he answers.

"What sort of game is this?" I ask. I'm almost casual thanks to the goodness of the rasta. "*This* is not professional."

"What game? What this?" Monarch says.

I tell him about Singh's visit. "So, what are you going to do about it?" I ask.

He says nothing, but I can feel his anger over the wire. He asks me to explain each detail of the evening. I do, then press for explanation. He admits to me that the real contact is stuck in Venezuela with the shipment and had no choice but to entrust the operation to his brother until he returns.

"If he comes near me again, I'm leaving. If anyone other than Mr. Venezuela calls, I'm leaving. I can't talk anymore; my throat is wrecked from being with him." I pause. Then the *last* coffin nail—"Do you have any idea how much cocaine that man smokes?"

There is silence on the line like the hush before a hanging—and with this last loaded question, I become the executioner.

I'm too tired to sleep, too tired to think. Exhaustion clogs my mind, and denies me precise thought—the very thing I need now, to strategize. I have to protect myself. I'm a belligerent witness to a botched job; my life is dear to no one but myself. Though less so now that I may have murdered Singh.

I'm wracked by angst. I roll in sweat-stained sheets behind double-locked doors, twisting myself in synthetic bedding until I am made a mummy. Motionless, I lay there staring out the window, a floor-to-ceiling blackness; it's impossible to see what's out there. I strain, but can make out only the dimmest imitation of myself, propped upon the black-paned casement. I wore, I wear, no watch, but am alone with the tick, the tock behind my eyes, that prop them open like picks, and open open OPEN, they see nothing but a mirrored outline, a reflection so nebulous as to make me question my genealogy. Neither homo nor sapient, but pythoned like a lamia, blood-sick as a vampire, harpy—oh I am that—greedy and grasping for an easy way out. Mortal only in my dreams, for I fear that this dread is infinite. Life taker, swill slayer. If you flap a butterfly's wings in China, the earthquake in Peru is on your hands.

I killed the wolf, and so shall I remain a pig. Oh cursed, cursed conscience, awakened too late, like a lazy, slacking slut—and now you've missed the bus.

And though my eyes view only dread, still I resist shutting them. Open-eyed pig, I feel along the wall of my pen in darkness, and inch my way through the night, exploring this nadir, into which, pushing myself, I've slid. The second's thrill of descent is long over. This far down, it's hard to move—it has to do with the pressures; people have died diving so deep. I struggle with, then settle into, my shroud of unmoving black, a pen populated by no living thing, save myself, an outline. So I begin again. I ignore the scratch of bedding that binds me and instead hold bottom to me like soft cotton wool, to pat the dampness of my fever, shield my open eyes from the glare of the unseen.

But a cocoon's time, if she is to live, is finite. And so the sun comes too soon. Its brightness draws my pupils into twin pricks of pain, I rise unwrapped and view the country's breathtaking beauty. Nothing could prepare me for the sight. Such things cannot be seen from the ground, nor through the low-level ceiling of night.

The mountains rise from the industrial slum triumphant—lush, pedestaled, but miraculously near, like a forest sprung up from a fountain—a high green upon the glass of beryl pond that seems to surround it, like a shrine. And all around, the glorious glitter of sky, an uninterrupted blue, splays rays upon the pane, now transparent to the colors beyond. I feel so small—a blade of grass up on that mountain. My God, that mountain was right next to my window. It had been there all along.

I feel helpless, alone, and happy—all at once. When the

full force of light is upon me, I finally doze off. My body lets go that last grip on itself and I fly off flapping, dreaming of orbits and mortal coils, rotations and roundabouts. They all spin so fast around me that I'm hesitant to jump on—like a child faced with a brazen merry-go-round stallion that spins past, teeth bared. You know the horse, the one with the sneer of defiance on its lip—the beautiful one.

෨

I awake startled, angel bones aching. I think of Crash and myself, light as feathers; neither of us left even the shallowest indent with our bodies. We always had back problems.

My mind replayed an old dream this morning, the same one I had after I came upon Crash passed out beside the CD player—no bottle in his hands, just blood. I'd run to the loo for a cloth, and saw dots, red and random, as if the paint from a miniaturist's brush had been flung in a fit of eyestrain, as if the artist had looked too long at his cramped fantasy. I'd wiped his blood, cried, then napped to be near him.

In the dream, he hovers from a great distance. I look up to see his silk coat glisten like a great star long past its sudden burst to billion times brightness. I long to wrap him around me, but far away, my own small star begins a collapse whose frantic rate will exceed his slow explosion. Then, from across the vast delta that separates us, comes a melody arranged by its very improvisation, dissonant and eternal—the spheres are singing. And the sound is lovely.

Just as it was.

It seems late now. I call the front desk for the time; after many rings—I stop counting after twenty—a voice says, "Noon." I call the phone by the Papaya Queen, thinking that I might still be able to catch Matthias. Her "grandson" answers—I call him "Six" now in perpetual apology after getting him mixed up one day with his younger brother; five is a near unforgivable insult. I tell Six that if he runs and wakes Matthias, I promise to sneak with him onto the beach at Sandy Lane and splash water on the lacquered hair of the women, "not the old women, only the young ones," I emphasize.

Six pauses on the phone; I can hear from his breathing that he's still weighing the deal.

"Okay, okay . . . I'll throw in a pineapple and ham pizza." I make gagging sounds; he laughs, agrees, and runs off. I hope that no one hangs up the dangling receiver that sways in the Bajan air—so much cooler than what awaits me outside this a.c. Lighter, too. Or so it seems. I listen to the island, I say hello to no one in particular, meaning thank you for letting me be both alone and accompanied; thank you for caring for me still—me who you should've spit into the sea. I envision the Papaya Queen's food stand nearby, and inhale fish smells through the wire. The fig tree on the other side of the road is dropping its unpicked bounty—I can tell by the unmetered thuds in the background. I hear island chickens clucking nearby, but no people. Then I hear dogs bay a barrier in the distance. *Damn.* I wonder if my gang will let the kid pass, but before I can worry too long, he comes back on the phone.

"Two pizzas. Jaws she take my roti," says Six.

"Roti? Where you get da roti? Doesn't your grandma

feed you good and you go an spend she money on the competition down the road," I say in the voice of the Papaya Queen, and cluck my tongue. Six is silent. I hear his frown, feel his shame. Six clips hotel hedges just so he can buy Colombian roses for the Queen. *Poor Six.* "No, I'm kidding, I'm *just kidding.*" I wonder about this word's etymology, if it entails extorting childhood. "I'll replace the roti, but not another pizza . . . and no splashing old ladies. Deal?" I am hard on old Six.

"Deal," he says and hands the phone over to Matthias. I tell him I miss him desperately—a sudden truth. I hear his smile; he's happy to hear from me.

"Why Port-of-Spain?" he says. "And why didn't you tell me before? I might have gone. My friend, a blond babe named Bettina, owns a store there—a batik boutique." He laughs, amusing himself. I write down the address.

I ignore his question. "Oh I . . . I'll tell all later," I say, knowing I won't. "So, you'll be at the airport?"

"If I get a pizza," he says.

I dress and venture out. Through the brass-handled double doors, heavy as a vault's, I wander unescorted to the street. I realize that no one from housekeeping awakened me. I couldn't find a "do not disturb" sign last night, so there was none hung to frighten maids away. The emptiness of the "full occupancy" hotel is beginning to unnerve me, but no bother, I'm off into the day. I'll go see Bettina. If she knows I exist, then maybe it won't be so easy for Monarch to erase me.

I walk the roadside and watch the convoy of workers' cars. Most—left parked below the stacks that processed the oil that made the gas that drove the droves toward the plants—have had their paint rotted off by chemicals. A sleek sedan with tinted windows races out ahead of the fleet toward me. I panic. *Monarch must have sent someone to clean up the mess.* The driver pulls up beside me. Running is out of the question—I can hardly breathe.

"Would you like the use of my car for the day?" he says. I stare at him. He's a moon-faced man, full of soft, strong light. I decide that he's not an assassin for Monarch, and hop in the car. "My name is Simon Singh," he says.

What is *in a name?*

"How much will this cost me . . . um . . . Simon?" I'm still breathing hard.

"Thirteen dollars. Sounds like you might not be in the shape for such a long walk to town. Is that where you're headed?"

"Yes. I guess." I show him the address of Bettina's Batik. "I'll give you fourteen dollars," I say, because thirteen is unlucky and I want to be free of omens.

We speed off; a split second sooner, later, and we'd have been hit from behind. Feathers fly like the dispersion of a cloud, a chicken truck veers away cursing. "It feels weird," I say.

Singh says nothing, but lowers the radio.

"I mean, a dollar always means a U.S. dollar. I feel like I'm responsible for something."

"You are," Singh says.

"For what?" I flick a feather.

"To give it away."

"Oh of course, the dollars—to you," I snide.

"No girl, the responsibility—to us," he chides.

"Oh, sorry," I say.

"Sorry a sorry word." Singh raises the radio and sings along. *If I was bright in school, I grow up to be a damn fool.* . . .

We pass shacks and stands, then pull up to a large building, box-shaped and windowless. Like a jail.

"Aren't we going to my friend's shop?"

"We here," he says.

"Yes?"

"Ain't ya never seen a mall, girl?" says Singh.

"Oh," I say. "Yes. No. Not for a long time."

"She's yours, from the States, ya know."

She? Storms, ships—and now malls. "Must you refer to it as a she?" I say. Then I see her; she appears from beneath the shimmer of hypnotic heat that surrounds the building. She's blond, two-dimensional and ten feet tall. She's a chain from the States. She's GAIL! and she salutes us, as if to say *check your judgment at the door and wave your grocery money goodbye.*

"Yikes!"

"Whassa madder girl?"

"Not a ting. Jus dat . . ." I catch myself slipping into his speech; he doesn't react, just looks straight ahead at the flaxen vixen and lets me keep his words.

"Looks like home," I say.

"You not really from the States," he says.

"I was. Where do you think I'm from?"

"Seem ta me you from nowhere," Singh says.

I'd like to stay with him. But I have to face the Gail. I slam the door, to ensure that Singh remains safe and separate from her.

"I'll wait here for you—but not too long, you know."

"I know," I say.

The mall is stifling. By the mouth where the sun hits the glass doors, it's an oven. There's no ventilation; the construction is for the advanced climate control that comes with modernity. The a.c. is off. I suspect it's to save money. The few shops near the entrance, Charlotte's Sugar Shack, Sid's Snack Shack, and Electric Shack, are closed. I assume GAIL! is open because of the cars parked beneath her. I suspect that, being an entity unto herself, she's cool. But I don't want to go there. I sip the last of my bottled water and seek out a trash can for the empty. There's one nearby, and a janitor beside it.

"Is it a holiday?" I ask.

"No." He looks like he sees a ghost.

"But there's no one here."

"I'm here," he says. I look at the gingerbread house growing mold in the window of Charlotte's, and I know it's time to drop some bread crumbs.

"I'm here too," I say, but he just keeps sweeping, and ignores me.

I mark that the way out is through the oven, and keep walking.

I walk past an open card shop, and a gated bookshop. I walk slowly until I see an array of multicolored needles proclaim Bettina's Batik across a white awning. It looks dangerous, but I can't see inside. I open the curtained door and a bell tinkles my arrival. I imagine this will be Bettina's cue to come to my rescue, and I pause before one of the many fans. It's cool inside the shop, and I'm relieved that, finally, I'll be known, and if lucky, missed.

But I'm met only by a glower, cower, and a stare. The three girls are everything, but none is blond.

"Bettina's not in," says Stare who sits sewing an African-inspired tunic. A cat nearby flicks its tail, awaiting my reply. Glower, splayed upon the white-tiled floor, cuts patterns. She is the likeness of Miss World, but low, so low to the ground.

"When will she be back?" I ask.

"Not today. Boss she gone to Miami."

"Do you know when she'll be back?"

"Best be by payday," says Stare.

"When's that?" I ask.

"Tree week."

"Oh. I'm a friend," I say, "I mean, my friend is hers." Glower no longer listens, Stare follows suit. My alliance scores not a whit, not a crumb. "That's pretty." I point to a gown embroidered with flowers and leaves. Cower nods. The garment is too stiff to sleep in, too translucent for town; it's leisure wear for the lady of the house. Ladies that never arrive, but have a driver deliver their pre-ordained dress to the hills. I realize that Bettina's has remained open because it doesn't rely on walk-in customers. The space itself is probably inexpensive—I'd bet the mall establishment was anxious to fill it. I'd bet Bettina is getting rich off the Ladies, the establishment, and Miss World. "I really need to speak with Bettina." Cower says nothing. "I'm from the States. I'm at the Happy Holiday Lodge." Cower nods again. *Speak to me,* I say. Then, "I'm sorry."

"Yes. I know," she says, and goes back to her batik. "Do you want to buy anyting?"

"Yes. No. Okay." I can't afford the batik. She hands me

a jumpsuit, all white. A nothing garment with minimum construction, no buttons, no zipper, just wrap and tie.

Glower on the floor tugs hard at a bolt of cloth; when the separation comes, it sounds like a whip. This, in turn, is answered by a crackle like thunder; the P.A. system has been turned on—and the notes of a too-familiar tune follow in downpour. I wonder if the janitor has done this for me, the lone customer. The thought of this makes me uneasy, the music uneasier still. It is, was, Crash's number one hit, "Something About Fate." The lyrics are banal. The volume is unrelenting. I have to go.

"Please tell Bettina to call Matthias," I say over the music. Stare doesn't accept the card that might leave record of me. I point to the small batik purse over the counter: Stare throws it in with the white, and I pay quickly with cash. The door, the song, tinkles as I close them, curtained, behind me.

Outside in the oven I remember that Matthias has no number.

Singh is still outside, his music is loud, but not monotonous.

"Do you want me to turn it down?"

"No," I say. "Please don't."

Back at the hotel, I call Jon and Elsa. They stand close to each other; I can tell by the static between their cordless phones, but can't bear to part them. I can hear well enough. They're disturbed I'm in Trinidad.

"Are you well?" says Elsa. She knew I wasn't, though not the extent.

"Fine," I say.

"Willa stopped by to see Pig."

"*What?*"

"She's spending a semester at Cambridge."

"Wow."

"She thought you'd be here, she's quite worried."

I'd put off calling her for just that reason. "Tell her I'm sorry, and that I'm proud of her. And give Pig a pat."

"Will do. Is Crash there then?" says Jon.

"*What?*"

"Give over. He's there—isn't he?"

"Only on the airwaves."

"Oh," says Elsa. "When you left we thought he followed you."

"Might have been tough," I said.

"Where were you luv?" says Jon.

I breathe deep. "Hospital."

"Bloody hell."

"Yes. Well, I'm out now."

"He left the band."

"What?"

"We worry," says Elsa. "He was using . . . again."

"I set him off," I say. Then left and never looked back. It's not until my mouth fills with salt that I realize I'm crying.

"The world set him off, *cheri*."

"You kept him in it."

"I don't know."

I never will know. Much later, Willa found through the Web that Crash had sackclothed his ass to a Spanish monastery, then gone on to new fame with a solo career in Australia. Sometimes situations show themselves through externals. Like when I was twelve and the ring I thought

I'd lost at school showed up on my brother's girlfriend. I let him—her—keep it. Back then the knowing was enough. Later I wanted redemption. I still do. But not everything in life brings redemption—if we're lucky we get just a taste. The rest is pretend, like a child's tea party. Substitute milk for tea, substitute dirt for sweets.

As for knowing, it's gotten easier. Still, I'd convinced myself Crash had left me, and he has, had, the moment my illness became apparent. But I went first.

I'd spent the last of our time hiding half-full bottles in couch cushions, car and house keys beneath carpets, while he slammed doors between us and wrote music, or drew slit notches up his arm, or wept. I wanted to believe the drug had stopped years ago. Heron, he'd called it. I thought of a great bird, a beauty that, to me, appeared flightless. Crash, with his gaunt elegance, his long legs, looked like this bird. When he was gone to intervals toured without me, he sent cards with gold-engraved pictures of two birds on the front. Herons, I thought, perhaps great blue. Inside, he was proud of his subtle allusion to monogamy, of one true mate. I didn't tell him his mistake, that he had them mixed up with swans. Later I found out he was right.

Since then, I never really thought he was gone for good. Not until now.

I write Crash a postcard, address it in care of his manager:

I'm in Trinidad. They play your song. I loved you. Goodbye.

The tense of the love is pretend, the parting, for real.

I lie on the dogwood bed and reach over to call room service. No one's home, so I flip on the tv. The only shows on are *Play Bridge with Paul Hackett!* and a revival from Port-of-Spain led by Jimmy Swaggart. I'm mesmerized by Jimmy's floor show.

"Let's all give. Give to God and pay for your sins," says Jimmy Swaggart. "And you, you there girl," he says to a beauty. "Get down on your knees and thank Jesus. I believe, I believe," he says, then snaps out of his trance. "I believe he's got a message for me to give to you." I wonder where Tammy Faye is—guess it's too hot for her; makeup runs within seconds in this climate—until I remember she belongs to the other televangelist. "And you out there—still clinging to your idols, your voodoo, your *witchcraft*. Hide your faces, hide them and repent. Who out there are heathen?" A few women stand up, look down. "Hell awaits you all," Swaggart says. "Hell is a heathen hotel, but you can't, I say you cannot check out." *Is this a dare?* "Come forth," he says. "Come forth and be saved." Three women come forward. They creep down the aisle, as if to their own executions. One by one they drop their bounty—beads, shells, and feathers—before him. Swaggart crushes the pile with a well-heeled shoe. One woman stifles a sob. They all give him dollars. He gives them a single bible to share, the size of a playing card.

Then there's the question of gods—tin from the altar or gold from the fleas.

I want the Swaggarts to go away, to go back to the States

to steal from people with cash enough to buy his rubber-coated relics—and their own phone line to call long-distance to his mechanized messiah.

I should go, too. I think maybe I've lured him here in the same way that a Seattlelite can bring rain to the crystal skies of New Mexico, or an Angelino brings drought to New York. But it's just guilt, grief, and ego—he'd been here long before me.

I switch to *Play Bridge with Paul Hackett!* thinking I can stave off despair with a rubber of camp, but Paul only bores me. I shut off the set, fearful that I might doze into a catnap into which Swaggart could creep.

I need a shower.

The shower doesn't seem to cool me, but I'm cleaner, except for my hair. I'm scared to wash it. I know it's a dead thing; still, I hoard parts of myself that might again come loose. I comb my tangle of colors into a ponytail, and look in the mirror: stray silvers surround the skin of a ten-year-old, uncreased save my eyes, crowed from swells and deflations. I'm shocked by this jumble of age, and can't believe that I'm either that young, or that old. I look closer. Brown, red, blond. Black, gray, white. I realize with some disappointment (and greater relief) that I won't grow to resemble my mother. I heave a great snuck-up sigh, a soul sneeze that seems to snuff some of Swaggart's brimstone, and I open my suitcase. I choose a black sheath that covers me well, and retains a certain elegance, despite its wrinkles. *A wreck*, my mother had said, *at least the boys won't bother you.* I'd worn it with Crash to a wedding in Soho. It's been balled up in my bag ever since. I'm not sure why I brought the dress; it's too hot for the Caribbean—plus it draws attention to my face. Sunglass marks around dark shadows.

I line up the cosmetic brushes (a gift from Polly, Thalia, and Clio) before me like dental instruments, to fill the abscess of my eyes. I dab white dots of concealer on the dark, rub bronzer over white; my face brightens. Last, I thumb through a ledger of tricks in my mind, and choose the most potent—red lipstick.

Apple excitation, strawberry alarm, or blood lust—these are the shades of power, Polly had instructed. *Puerto Rican pink may be pretty, but it's a bend-over color, never forget that.* And I didn't. But I did suspect a mouth that could scorch others might also starve itself.

It's almost past dinner. I walk downstairs to work up an appetite, and my heart, glad to be worked by physicality and not some shock of the mind, rewards me with the blush I forgot to apply. A poor man's Omar Sharif smiles at me from across the buffet. I make the mistake of smiling back. "An American!" Omar shouts, and runs to me. Great. I've been exposed as a Yank in a place still pissed over Grenada. "My mother was American." Omar speaks with a French accent. "My name is Arto Fauchi. My father was Egyptian," he says, as if to explain the Italian surname. My head spins. I need a drink.

"Scotch, single malt," I say to the server.

"Why does a beautiful woman choose such an arrogant drink?" asks Arto.

"To get to the other side?"

"Well, have whatever you wish, on me; this is my hotel."

I tell him about the nonexistent service and lost reservations.

"Accept my apology," he says. "Your suite will be my treat—I'm the Happy Holiday Honcho for the Caribbean and Venezuela."

"Cheers," I say. And mean it. Like a fisher adrift, I'd reeled in a real heavy.

I pick at the buffet. The scotch dulled my taste, and besides, the shrimp looks as if it's been exposed to desperate cryogenics. The shells on the near-extinct Caribbean lobster are brittle. The scallops are gray. I settle for rice, beans, and hearts of palm.

"You've never been kissed," Arto says. I set my fork down; it must be the red of my unsmeared opening that so persuades. "You're a virgin," he says.

" 'Fraid not," I say, and slug down the last of the scotch.

"No, you just think you've been touched." I smile at his implication, at the bullshit I've stumbled high-heels into. He takes my smile as license. "How about an after-dinner drink?" he says. I've yet to eat. "I'll get you a Calvados that's *almost* better than sex."

"I'll just stick to scotch," I say.

"The Calvados is divine—and I'm quite adept."

"I prefer not to mix." He takes his time ordering my next drink; it arrives well after his snifter. I'll have to try not to offend Arto. I need him for reasons I barely understand.

"It's fate. We've been brought together by fate."

"Hm."

"We're really royalty that have emerged here, in these forms. Everything has a reason."

"Of course."

"I'm a direct descendent of Nefertiti's, so you must have been too," he says.

"She was black, you know."

"Oh no, she was quite light, like gold dust."

"Oh—I guess I'm mistaken." I don't insist on the truth, and feel, in this failure, like a jailer who's let a clean man rot. Just to appease. I must be careful to appease. "I've never met an Egyptian," I say.

My toes peak naked through my sandals. Arto focuses on them. "I've been alone too long," he says, as he sips from his tiny fishbowl. I have an idea, and Arto, with his past-scotch hauteur, just might fall for it.

"My ex-fiancé is following me," I say. "I'm afraid he'll see us, and think you've disgraced his honor."

Arto nods.

"I'm afraid what he might do to you," I say, then add, looking around for effect, "He's Colombian."

I hope that this will appease Arto. I stack the odds, toss out a sure bet—but the coin lands on its edge.

"It's not safe to go back to your room," Arto says, "you must come to mine." He orders an employee to allow only those with a room key and proper identification past the lobby. Then he motions me toward the elevators. I don't know what else to do; it's late, too dark to find my own way, so I follow. He keys up to the penthouse, and my empty stomach plunges with the ascent.

I can't see the mountain from Arto's suite. I guess we're facing the wrong direction, because there's great visibility from atop the tower. I can see workers celebrating the end of their shift; a drink and a dance by Dumpsters in the back lot.

"I like Calypso," I say.

"Uckk, that muck."

"*Calypso* means truth."

"Yeah—well, I prefer tango." Arto's heels click discordant across fake marble floors, a flairless Astaire.

"Did you work in Argentina?" I ask.

"Oh no—though I'd have liked to. No, just here and Caracas. And before that the Cairo Hilton."

"How'd you end up here?"

"I left the Hilton—I was uncomfortable with the workers."

"Why?"

"I didn't like looking so much like those beneath me," he says. "I'm happier here—but still alone. The Trinis are scum. And the Indians should be sent back in boxes. Done away with like the real ones."

"Genocide?" I say.

"Hmmpf. The Arawak were animals," he says. I wonder if it was Arto who'd tried to build a Happy Holiday Lodge atop the site where Columbus's crew had raped four Arawak, then slit them like sheep. Legend is, the lone woman killed crew members while her intestines spilled out like angry eels. "They're not like *you*," Arto says. "I have *you* in my heart."

I change subjects, ask him about his family.

"My mother was a saint," he says. He sighs, relaxes, reclines on his couch. Arto is lanky and unfit; I imagine great knobs of elderly knees beneath his pants; I don't want to think about what else is hidden. He reaches into a bowl of peanuts on the end table and begins to crack. He pops the nuts into his mouth while he continues to talk. "*Virginia* peanuts," he says, as if they were Beluga. I dislike peanuts.

Arto lets the shells drop, he tries, inattentively, to keep them to one section of the table. The tiny clouds of peanut dust make my nose itch. He offers, but I refuse—they have the color of something dead.

Arto's room is pastel, the color of babies' bruises. Although it's a cavernous double suite I feel as if the ceiling's slowly being lowered on me, so I sit on the floor, look up, and listen to a prostrate man praise his mother.

An old adage comes to mind: "A man who so loves his mother will *not* pursue sex." I relax a bit—then a newer saying intrudes: "A man who so loves his mother experiences *endless* pursuit (of sex) with little enjoyment." At this, I shiver and stiffen as if one after the other, a country of mothers walks the site of my grave.

"Where's she from?" I ask.

"Graves End," he says. "In Brooklyn." I breathe in hard, hit by the accident of old neighborhoods.

"I was born in Brooklyn," I say.

"Oh—a sister," he says. "A *sister*." He unbuttons his shirt, arches his neck over the arm of the couch and dangles his head. His eyes bulge and I wonder if blood will overcome him. *"Mom,"* he murmurs, and runs his hands atop his body in appreciation.

I focus on a crack in the ceiling. He groans, he gropes. I stare into the plaster. I'm mostly in the plaster. I hope that my silence shields what remains. But if not, I'll need the elevator key. I panic and look back.

The key is on the end table and Arto is exposed.

I could escape into the spray of gunfire that may await me beyond the lobby, or I could stay silent, still, untouched. But neither happens.

Arto lunges at me like a vampire arisen from a series of bloodwet dreams. I make a small sound, more revulsion than pain. He runs his hands over my dress, and gasps. "My sister, my mother." I half expect someone, perhaps Polanski, my countryless compatriot, to appear and save me. No one does. I slip away, crawl across the floor. He grabs my sandal. I toss it. He doesn't press, he doesn't coax; he doesn't try to entice me with his aforementioned skills, instead he catches hold of my leg, and on the curve of calf made naked by the tumble, he rubs himself. I stop my struggle, and look toward the window. I see the landing lights of planes—and try to envision their crash. A hundred bodies fallen from the sky, bashed and burned, their travelers long freed, while the world tries to piece together toes and hair and teeth. I find solace in this fragmented phantasm—these forms left behind. Trash from ash, and lust to dust.

I think of kicking, but I do nothing; I reason that I'm intact, that it's only an appendage. Perhaps I'll limp, but I will live. Arto moans and pants. I feel his heat, imagine his white seethe inside and spread throughout, infecting me with a tetanus that will lock my body, corrode my heart.

"Oh . . . Mother," he says. He's finished. And I am freed.

I wobble barefoot to the window, where I hope to see empties and ash, but down below, illuminated by the lights of the pool, I see a girl and a boy hold hands, and kiss.

"Ah, you are my darling," Arto gasps from behind me. And he means it.

I shake the shells from my sandals. Arto gives me the elevator key and I walk out.

The mountain is invisible at night. But I'm alive, and soon it will be light enough to leave. I pick up the phone and, dialing in darkness, I conjure Monarch. "I won't stay," I say.

"Wait," he says. I say nothing. "Wait, just wait. Please." He orders, threatens, pleads.

"I don't want to wait. I have no money to pay the hotel bills," I say, though I assume they've been waived.

"But your advance," he says.

"My advance was shit; I won't stay here and use it up."

"Wait," he says.

"You haven't paid me enough."

"I will."

"You can't. I'm sick of this; I don't want to wait any more." This time I yell.

"*C'mon*, it's not so bad," he says. His voice brightens, like a dull star that my anger illuminates. I tell him that Waiting is Hell and he's the Devil, then I hang up.

Of course I know better; I know that waiting's the devil and he's just a Harvard grad who loves money. And hell. Well, hell is having your leg humped by a racist moaning *mom*—when close by, there are lovers illuminated.

❧

I make my getaway at dawn—restaurant and hotel employees are notoriously late risers and I want to avoid Arto. I walk past reception, out those massive, now unguarded, doors. Then stop, and turn back. I have to return the keys, mine and his. I don't want any souvenirs. I've rinsed the dress and left it for the maid.

The receptionist hands me a computer printout. "What's this?" I say.

"Your bill," she says.

"But it's been paid."

"Whatever gave you that idea?"

"Shit." I examine the bill. Arto signed the first night—but left me in debt for last night's rut. I hand over my credit card, but the machine refuses it so I'm forced to pay with cash. What I have left won't provide me room and board for more than a week in the States, except maybe in the motels of one-hour adulterers and mad bombers. I fold the money, filthier than before, into my pocket, making it go Murphy, out of sight.

"Have a nice trip home," says the receptionist.

"Thanks," I say and walk away. As an afterthought I leave my address, if you could call it that (St. James, B'dos c/o Turtle Research) and tell her to give it to Arto. Monarch might try to kill me. I figure it's better to leave evidence with the enemy than to pass inconspicuous as mist, no sicker than the rest.

Outside, just past the blue, I can see the sky being whitewashed by a yawn of light. I look up high, like a tourist in Manhattan. This is a dangerous thing to do. But I'm okay, intact, so I arch further, my neck just a breath from snapping. I see islands in the clouds, and just beyond, in cumulus reminder, I follow the shape of a familiar peninsula to its continent. I think of my home—a great mass that thinks it's better than its southern twin, perhaps because it believes it lies above. The North ignores the directionless topography of spheres—the way orientations migrate—and even poles can begin to melt away.

I walk through the gates with my prisoner's wages. I check for my ticket, hail a cab to the airport, and wish for the best. In crossing boundaries there's always change; it's always irreversible. In crossing boundaries, you—as you know yourself—die. I suppose that's why people don't want to go there.

I dread running into Monarch. But avoidance of Barbados will be no safer in the long run than outright exposure. I fly back to fly forward. And forgive myself. I pop no pills. I don't fret, I don't itch. I have more pressing matters to attend to—for one, Six awaits his pizzas.

The overheads shake; the seatbelt light blinks; my drink spills. I hold on and laugh. The De La Renta-ed Dominican woman across the aisle looks at me as if I've grown yams on my head. I don't care, I'm high with the thrill of motion. "It's just like People's Express," I say.

"Communist," she mutters.

I shake my empty cup at the steward. "I'm parched."

De La Renta's still fuming.

"Don't you care about your life?" she says.

"Life?" I say. "Life's a bowl of white-knuckled freedom."

When the plane drops, not so unexpectedly, I sing with the Dead. Jerry croons his postcoma "Touch of Gray." I offer De La Renta the headphones, but she waves me away like a bad smell.

The plane lands with a small sideways skid, a demure concrete curtsey. The air is thick with morning heat. It's the time of day to sleep through if you can. I walk to immigration. Percival's there waiting, as promised. I kick my bag to the side with my Lone Ranger boot. He picks it up, dusts it off.

"Thanks, Perce. My friend should be here soon with my ticket."

"Don dig nuttin'," he says. "Did you like Tobago?"

"What? Oh—yes. I met a nice rasta." There's one asleep in front of a nearby fan, I watch as a guard kicks him awake. "Trini rastas have it worse," I say.

"What you mean?" says Percival.

"Well, here they're tolerated more."

"Hmmpf."

"Why do they bother you?"

"Rasta spout all sort a nonsense."

"Like what? Is it because they smoke ganja?"

"Yeah right sure. No. No," he says, then asks, "Got some?"

"No. *Lord no.*"

"Don't," he says.

"Don't what?"

"Take da Lord's name in vain."

"How do you know it was?" I say. Percival's confused. "Rasta god is nature, or something like that, right?"

"You believe dat god is flyin' fish? Breadfruit tree?"

"I don't know."

"God, he make you in his image. Now, you don' look like no flyin' fish to me."

"I don't look like god either. I'll tell you the truth, Perce—I'm not sure I want to see what god looks like."

Percival stands silent by the window; outside light bends on jet fumes, and all the world looks wavy.

"Oh Perce, I think maybe men get god mixed up with things—religion, drugs . . ."

He steps back, as if I might be dangerous.

"But, a friend once told me that I was kissed by god."

"We all are. Girl, we special all."

"Yeah, but he left hickeys on me."

"*What?*"

"Nevermind." Percival's back at the window; he makes no motion to address me further. But the silence, the light, is too much.

"Are you Jewish?" he says.

"Don't know. My mom says I'm Israeli." Percival shuffles his shoes.

"Some rastas aren't real. Some just like women, ganja, and they hair."

"And the others?"

"They like god. I mean nature."

"How can you tell the difference?" I ask.

"It hard ting."

"Yes," I say.

"History make em so," he says.

"The trees?"

"*No*. Da rasta." Percival scans to see if anyone's listening. I feel like I'm about to be given a password. "Long time past, da English girls, dey come to islands to sleep with black mon, but we Bajan like whine wid our own. So dey go rasta. Soon da rasta become known for dat. An everyone believe dat if you rastafarian . . ."

"Then you studded for the British," I said.

"Uh—yes," Percival says. The rasta moves closer to the fan. The guard swings his nightstick.

"I'd bet the Christian men, black and white, slept with the English girls too. Just not out in the open."

"No madder—nobody whine like dat no more. But fake rasta on beach still primpin for ghosts. I sorry," he says.

"Don't be silly," I say. He laughs and says he likes the way I say "silly"—like his baby sister when he sticks his tongue out at her. He excuses himself and brings back coffee sweet with evaporated milk.

"I feel bad that you're waiting so long," I say. Matthias is late. I worry, but not too much. It's early for him. Percival and I revel in the coffee. But minutes gather expectantly behind us, like a crowd of unfed children. "We should phone." I hope Six is around to answer, and not too miffed with me. I should never have shamed him—I should have given him something useful, like rage.

"You can't." He points. The phone booths are beyond immigration. "But I will. What da number?" I panic; I don't remember. Then realize it's in my bag. Each time I leave a place, if only for a week, I return, forced to relearn basics.

"Ask for Matthias," I say. "If a boy that answers to Six picks up the phone, make sure to promise him two pineapple pizzas—if you don't I'll be here forever."

I wait and wait. I watch two flights unload. Something must be wrong. Percival should be back by now. Maybe Matthias met up with fellow Germans, got drunk and forgot me. Maybe he's been hurt, or arrested. Maybe his habit of smoking in bed had, without me there, caught up with

him, and destroyed my ticket home. Maybe his auto-
graphed photo of David Hasselhoff was in ashes—a pleasant thought, but bad timing. Or maybe Six was simply
negotiating for more junk food.

Percival returns red-faced. "Well?" I say.

"I speak to Six." Percival won't look at me.

"What did he say?"

"Well . . . it was hard to understan he—Six speak wid
mouth full. I offer da pizzas an he run right 'way to fetch
Matthias. Long time pass before Six come back."

"Six came back." I'm relieved. "So . . . Matthias is on
his way."

"Well, not so. But Matthias come soon, yes, come soon."

"What did Six say?"

"Six *ask*, not say."

"What? He told me two pizzas was enough."

"I think you Americans have problem with pizza. Six
ask," Percival looks away, ". . . why Matthias hurt Marcia."

"Matthias hurt Marcia?!"

"No."

I need more coffee. "Were they fighting?" Percival
doesn't answer. "Fisticuffs," I say.

"No. No fisticuff. I think maybe Six walk in on some
whinin; I think maybe someone need tell Six about the
birds and the bees. I try to, but . . ."

"Oh good Lord."

"Don't—"

"Sorry," I say. "Naked?" He nods. "On *the bed?*"

"Yes."

"Aw Jesus. Sorry, *sorry*," I say. *My* bed, is what I'm
thinking. Percival's disturbed. I suppose he wonders where
I expect whinin should take place.

"Are they coming now?" I ask. He flushes. We sit and wait, awkward witnesses to the loss of innocence. *Poor old Six.*

The rapid flap of sandaled feet breaks my reverie of regret. We come face to face with the culprits. They look younger than I remember them; I'm afraid to see what Six looks like. "Where's Six?" I say.

Matthias shrugs. Marcia smiles.

I say something that makes absolutely no sense. "What in god's name were you doing up that early?"

"We're up because of you!" they say.

"Oh. Nevermind."

Percival tries not to stare. I can tell he expected a different couple—not the man-eating Marcia and androgynous Matthias.

"Thanks man," Matthias says, and hands him the ticket.

"Hiya Percy," says Marcia. I guess she knows him from the airport because she's a tour guide.

"Hi Pookie girl." No. The dialogue's a bit too familiar. They must have been school chums. But not lovers—the look on Percival's face clearly states that he, a hulking man of a man, has been rejected as such by Marcia.

I feel an overwhelming tenderness toward Percival, and see him suddenly as a hero. I want to comfort the big lug, to take his head in my lap and tell him about the changing role of evolution—that physical strength just can't support a woman like it had in the past—that it's smarts you need, that smarts are big, that studies say only children who've been breastfed have them, and that men with feminine traits and women with masculine traits are the smartest of all. Then I'd tell him I'm stuck with being clever, that wisdom eludes me, that I'd been fed formula, and dropped on my head by a brother. But it's ten A.M. and Percival's already had a hard day. So instead I say, "How about coming out for pizza with me and Six tomorrow?" Percival looks at Matthias; he could snap him like a swizzle stick.

"Ire," he says.

૭

Somehow Marcia has procured a car. I want to ask her if it's the professor's but don't want to intrude. I want to ask what, if anything, happened to the professor, and how Matthias happened. But I don't. It seems natural that we three should be here like this, though I feel a slight discomfort in their afterglow. I'm glad we're going to Marcia's and not back to my, our room.

I'd never been to Marcia's before. Mostly I believe this was due to the relationship between Marcia and her mother. The few times I phoned her, I heard scolds in the background. Because Six often stood vigil at the pay phone, one particularly cacophonic call was comprised of Marcia listening more to Six's cries for Coca-Cola than to me—while I, in turn, heard a slap that lessened her own voice. I didn't call much after that; I was too busy making mistakes. But now Marcia's mother has gone to visit relatives in Guyana, and I've made enough mistakes to hold me for a while.

We pull up to a chattel at the foot of the great hill in Christ Church, the hill where dobermans roam—a hill with gates and mostly white inhabitants. Marcia has lived beneath this hill all of her life. Her home, I discover, once inside, is a photonegative of itself.

I know that Marcia doesn't have money. She gets by on wiles not means, but her surface is all elegance. The surface of her home is all splinter, all suffer—yet inside lies both modernity and comfort. There are Persian rugs piled one atop the other, their slight stains and small frays do little to hide their lineage. There is, unbelievably, a Tiffany lamp atop an ancient dresser; there is a thirty-four-inch television, a vcr, and a complete stereo console. There are myriad tapes and albums, and a lesser amount of videos. I wonder if Marcia is involved in import/export. Then I realize hers is not so different from most Bajan households; almost all have vcrs. But none have Persians. Marcia has so many. The little house is cramped.

Wardrobes overflow from Marcia's bedroom out into the living room. They're stuffed with clothing that, upon closer inspection (a few dresses have been hung hurriedly inside out) I can see she's made herself; I spy a footpedal Singer, pushed against a wall, in confirmation. Above the machine there are framed reproductions of Coco Chanel sketches. Coco came from poverty, yet refused to thread a needle— perhaps doing for herself was a mistake Marcia had made.

Marcia is happy beneath the hill, her smile fills the little house in an instant; there is no interference by Mother, no slap in vain to a face on which shame will not stick. The roses outside must be difficult for Marcia to cultivate in such a climate, but bloom they do.

Matthias is happier than I've ever seen him.

"Panther girl," he pokes me. "Vat you did down there? Silly panther girl, broke out from nothing. Your bars ain't your bones." He sticks out his tongue. I growl at him, make a claw of my hand, but he grabs my wrist. "Ah, she hass much heat today." He licks the air with his still-extended tongue, and threatens me with saliva.

"Gross. Well, at least I know where it's been," I say. Marcia, Matthias, and I all stick out our tongues, then we see whose can reach farthest down our chins. Marcia comes close, but I win. The strain of days is vanquished by this match. We're together in celebration of this hot morning (they've had sex, I escaped death). We're monstrous children home without parents. We don't need to ask each other what to do; we just proceed. Marcia rummages in the kitchen and boils a big pot of water. Matthias rolls a large fragrant spliff. I lie on the floor, a pillow beneath my head, and study the ceiling; I don't seek a crack to escape through, and anyway it's tin. Marcia smells the spliff from across the house. "You better leave some of my special macaroni and cheese for us, you big banana head," she says to Matthias, then she begins to sing. Matthias answers Marcia with his own hums; their voices, an ocean apart, sound symphonic. My mouth waters. I'm overwhelmed by the cooking smells; the kitchen is just beyond the living room, the same room really—only the two bedrooms and one tiny bathroom, narrow as a broom closet, have doors. Matthias and Marcia continue singing. I'm caught in the middle; their currents wash over me, and I float atop the salt-dense flood of sexual innuendo. When it subsides, I see Matthias sort through the videos. "How about horror?" he says.

"Oh yes," says Marcia.

"Fine by me." Horror suits us all. Matthias and Marcia, because it's an excuse to cuddle, and myself because tel-evised atrocities are always comforting after you've faced real demons.

Matthias curates. I swipe the spliff, toke intently, and muse on this homeopathy of emotion. I smell the burble of spices and cheese—and I feel safe. A temporary illusion, sure, but that's what celebrations are for.

"*The Exorcist* or *Rosemary's Baby*?" says Matthias.

Marcia stops stirring to consider.

"Well, that priest in *The Exorcist*—he's a babe," I say.

"Dimi? *Eew.* Too old. Maybe if he had a son or something," says Marcia.

"Well, *The Exorcist* is scary. . . ." I say.

"Pea soup could ruin our appetites. . . ." says Marcia.

"Und raw liver?" says Matthias.

"What about it?" she says.

"Rosemary eats it," I say.

"Oh yeah, but not until much later in the movie. We'll be finished by then."

"Vell, I like *Der Exorcist*," Matthias says. Marcia looks at me for some reaction; she's a gracious hostess.

"*The Exorcist* makes me sad. *Rosemary's Baby* has such an uplifting ending." I blow smoke rings from atop the rug's caress, and imagine its colors kissing me like little kittens.

"*Vhat?*" Matthias says.

"I mean, through the whole movie the girl has no clue what's going on in that skinny little bod of hers. Well— after all that tension, the internal is finally made external." At this moment, I have an epiphany of relief, gratefulness even, for my own unsubversive ailment. "*And then*, and then she accepts what's alien as her own, and realizes that what is other belongs to the self. Yeah, yeah. *Yes.*" I toke some more.

When I look up, I see that all action has ceased and the pair is discussing me between themselves, like parents faced with a profligate child. Matthias marches over, snatches the spliff, pauses, slaps my wrist as an after-thought, and returns to the vcr. "Okay, *Rosemary's Baby*."

"Yes, then we can be glad we don't live in the Dakota," says Marcia. She stirs more spices into the glop, lowers the gas, and comes to me with a cold Banks beer—as if in consolation for Matthias's deprivation.

"Ah, breakfast beer," I say, "liquid gold."

"*Mar-see-ya*," says Matthias.

"Oh chill out, Matthias, you know Bajan beer's weak." (The alcohol content *is* low, as if brewers know to weigh in the intoxication already present in island air.)

"It's just that you don't look so good," he says. "You looked better before you decided to go island-hopping."

"I'm just tired, I'll be okay. Really, all is well," I say and sip. "Mm. Mm. Yeast soda—full of vitamins." It does taste nourishing. I didn't realize how parched I was. Flying is drying. But with a sip of Banks, and a deluge of kindness from the lovers close by—I'm quenched.

"Food's ready," Marcia yells triumphantly from the kitchen. She sets out a crusted yellow pepper sauce bottle freckled red, and hands me the watery island catsup (it's too thin to call ketchup).

"None for me—I like it hot," I say, and grab the pepper sauce. "Wow, a new bottle." I admire its plentitude.

"You gonna drink up all my pepper sauce?"

"No." I size it up. "Just half."

Marcia thinks my consumption unnatural. I use pepper sauce all day long. I dump it on oatmeal, or eggs if they're available; splash it on sandwiches until it leaks out the sides, staining my hands. The area beneath my nails is aurulent, perpetually peppered.

The Papaya Queen likes real mustard, made from mustard seeds, but she never bothered me about my strange habit. She must have known the reasons. I only knew I wanted cayenne. Food without it wasn't worth eating (except island chicken). I ate; I gained weight. The weight allowed me to survive, but it was the sauce that made me live.

The secrets of the sauce were revealed years later, by my roommate, a health nut named Lorraine who didn't touch cheese sandwiches. *Puh-lease, no dairy*, was her refrain. (The fear of lactose intolerance was endemic in those years that found *any* maternal influence suspect.) I came home one day to find Lorraine stirring cayenne into a glass of water. "You're *not* going to drink that—are you?" Lorraine plopped a few ice cubes and a celery stick in. "At least have some of my vodka with it. It's triple-filtered." (Lorraine's holisticism stopped for alcohol, as long it wasn't made with wheat or yeast.)

"It's for *the blood*, to purify *the blood*," she said.

"What?"

"Pepper, *red* pepper. Black and white are bad; they can build up," she said in a conspiratorial tone. "Red purifies the blood." She paused, then spoke as if to a child. "Red cleanses blood of any bad stuff." Then she swigged down all but an inch of brew in two gulps. I sized up the amount; it came to much less than a breakfast serving.

"Oh my God."

"C'mon, it's not that bad." She gave me the glass.

"Thanks for the dregs," I said and finished them. "No. It's not that bad. It's beautiful. It's wondrous."

౿

I felt that day as if an angel, hidden amongst the bombed-out ruin of my past, had crawled out dusty and sheepish to reveal itself. I wanted to thank someone; I thanked the Papaya Queen silently. I realized that keeping me in pepper sauce had cut her profit considerably. But it was my own body—older, sagging, still spackled, ever sagacious—that I owed my existence to.

In America, in wellness, when the occasional doctor will beg reasons for my survival with the spite of a jealous relation, I will answer only—pepper sauce, Lottie's.

"I already put a lot of pepper in." Marcia tries to halt my depletion of her newly bought bottle of Lottie's.

"You put white pepper in." I guess at this, knowing white pepper to be a Bajan staple in macaroni dishes.

"So—you don't appreciate my cooking."

"No. Yes. I do." I blow a kiss. "I like white pepper, but I don't crave it like you do that cheeky kraut." Marcia snaps a dishtowel at me and places the steaming bowl on the kitchen table. The starter's pistol of cold beers pops, and we're off. Matthias and I run to the grub in a competition that culminates in stasis, mouths full, before the screen. We stare at the streets of New York, full of witches, and I feel a pang akin to seeing a child you've given up, now grown. The Dakota dissolves into frame.

"Don't fall for it," mumbles Marcia.

I don't last long; I'm full and the feeling of eyes shut before a television, having guests inhabit your own too-incestuous consciousness, is so pleasant that I drift off. I dream that I take bitter tea with Ruth Gordon. It makes me stronger, gives me visions. Ruth narrates the slide show in my head, then tells me that contempt for and fear of a woman's body is great for box office.

∽

I awake to dusk; the screens, both in my mind and on the set, have been long dark. I stretch, still sluggish from so much starch, unbutton the top of my now-tight shorts and waddle through the shallows of oncoming evening to Marcia's bedroom. The door is cracked. The lovers sleep, their bodies a braid. I go in search of the same.

I hope to catch a bus to Peter's, not to save time, but perhaps myself. I shouldn't be out alone; Monarch might be waiting. No buses come. I walk north on the main road. There's no shoulder on the other side, so I can't face oncoming traffic. Cars on the road pass infrequently, but still, the whiz of each passing vehicle unsettles me. I think of walking the coast. It's indirect and the sand will slow me down, but I like the idea—of facing the crash of waves, rather than being hit from behind. It's quite a distance with all the twists, but I know if I can sustain the rhythm of motion, everything will be fine. At least while I'm walking.

I leave the main road and make my way toward the shore, past the hedge-lined roundabout of a hideaway hotel bordering Christ Church and St. Michael. It seems out of the way, too mid-range for Monarch. Guests step from taxis and wait for baggage. A lot of them are young women like myself. At a distance, a haircut and clothes seem the only disparity. One girl paws at a gold-enameled compact, and powders her nose. The tiny cloud muddies immediately upon contact. "Nothing will hold here," I say. Her friend, in a tie-dye shirt and tennis skirt, approaches me.

"Are you staying at this hotel?" She speaks loudly over her walkman.

"I'm just passing through. But I've been here before. Now I live way up the coast."

"I think I'll just stay down here this trip."

"The sea's like glass here," I say.

"Yes. Safe," she says.

"What's that your listening to?"

"D'Arby."

"D'Arby who?"

She looks confused, like her outfit. "Don't you know?"

"Know what?"

"Terence Trent D'Arby—he's the hottest! Been number one on the charts now for two weeks." I can hear the faint, familiar buzz. *Stay, ay, ay.* The king is dead. Long live the King. At least for a few more weeks.

The powdered friend is impatient. "I'm famished. Thirsty, too," she says.

"Joseph's is just south of here, in St. Lawrence Gap. They've got great food—it's not English. And there's a club nearby that serves girls free rum punch tonight, but be careful . . ." I say. My arm is yanked hard from behind. I turn, still smiling, a true island citizen who knows the importance of happy tourists, and I see him.

"Back so *soon* . . ." Monarch hisses. He stops when he sees the girls.

"I told you I was leaving." My elbow aches, my hands tremble. The girls wave and walk away. "Mining for Americans here . . . huh?" My voice catches in my throat like a shot bird. "I'll be missed." Monarch laughs. I take aim with names, specific as bullets. "Marcia Waverly," I say. He laughs again. "Peter Rock," I say. Monarch flinches— then laughs. "The Papaya Queen."

"Who?"

"The old woman who runs the food shack in upper St. James." Monarch looks scared. But he pulls at me again. The other guests, the men, take notice of my distress and his aggression, but they see the cut of his suit, sense a prior relationship (he's a man, and I'm a woman), and so they pretend to see nothing at all. Except one man, a lone porter, who, at the mention of the Papaya Queen, approaches warily. Monarch smiles widely at him. But the porter, steely gray and years past bribery, ignores this.

"I think you better leave," the porter says. He stares at Monarch; it seems they've seen each other before. "I can't break you mon, but I *can* make your evening miserable if you don't go." I cradle my left forearm gingerly like a wounded infant, and the baggage man leads me gently away by the other shoulder. The crowd views us in disapproval—we're a smudge on their postcard.

The old man and I disappear to the back porch of the hotel. We sit for awhile in silence.

"Tell your grandma I said hi," he says.

"Yes. I will. I have to go now. Thank you." He watches me disappear up the coast. Over the lapping of waves, I think I hear him say, "Keep walking."

I muse on the mention of the Papaya Queen as incantation. I speak her name aloud to the waves, and wonder if I'll see her tomorrow. The thought of her greasy fishballs makes my stomach ache, but I want to see her. I'll pass her home on the way to Peter's, I could drop by. But I know that, like a seer Evelyn Wood, she'll read me in an instant, send me back on my way to Peter, and scold me for stopping. "Ole stick o' fire don take long to catch," she'd say.

Three miles must have passed; I can see the lights of Bridgetown. *Keep walking.* I still feel the urge to look over my shoulder, but don't. Somewhere along the way, fear must have strayed from me, slipped off to take a piss in the scrub where runaways crouch, lonely and shivering. I walk the sands of the Hilton, and look up toward the veranda. I see guests huddling together, hear the clink of their glasses, the tinkle of dinner music. I walk farther, humming Bob Marley and Pink Floyd.

The latter was one of Six's favorites, he laughed at me when I sang the former. "Ughh, you're like my mum, or grandma, even." To antagonize him further I sang Sparrow songs.

"He's your Sinatra," I'd said.

"Who Sinatra?" I danced a figure eight lasciviously; he giggled and squinched his nose. "And why you like old man?"

"Now you sound like *my* grandma," I said.

"Why so?" I didn't tell him about the life-size poster of my childhood idol, Einstein, that hung in my bedroom and caused my grandmother such grief.

Why you like old man? Why out of all the granddaughters in the world, god gives me you—a grave-robber.

God don't play dice Grandma.

And you—stop telling god what to do. Ah misere me.

✺

"My grandma thought I wanted to whine old men," I told Six.

"Eeew," he said, not sure what it meant. "So, do you?"

"No."

"But Sparrow?"

"Hey, he's different—they don't call him 'Mighty' for nothing."

"Eeew," said Six.

I had walked myself into better thoughts, gaining so much momentum that I almost pass Peter Rock's. But his dogs alert me.

"Hello," I say to them—they smile, but are confused as to why I steal in the dark, like the intruders they're trained to keep at bay. They dig with elegant claws in the sand and look around as if to ensure they're not being observed, then they come noses cold and bestow kisses earnestly—if not in the random, sloppy manner of my own pack.

"I thought I tell you not to bewitch my dogs."

Peter stands stolid before me. The pups pant beside me, still smiling. A twist surfaces on Peter's face and I brace myself, thinking he's about to yell at me, the dogs, or both. But instead, he grips my shoulders, retreats, then grips again. This goes on for a while—a kind of check by him to see that I'm solid—until he collapses around me, and I melt beneath him.

"What happen' to you," he says, as if he knows.

"You need a haircut." I think of my own close shave and begin to cry.

"Don dig nuttin babe," he whispers. He kisses my eyes, presses until I see white. I feel as if an overhead's been flipped on to dissolve my nightmare. Peter removes his t-shirt and wipes my tears with it. I smell time, his day retained in cotton. It's grit and work and dogs and salt. It's life. Peter dabs and swabs, then puts the shirt aside. The tears have vanished, save for the few escapee drops that mingle indistinguishable in the sweat that slides between my breasts and gathers in rivulets down my stomach.

Peter keeps his mouth pressed to mine. I feel like I've been too long in the sea, I hear buzzing. Like I've swallowed wildlife. I wonder if I've stopped breathing.

Peter thrums my flesh with outstretched palms—as if in a surrender preceding the charge of calvary. He thrusts fingers in flesh, up toward my center. His hands, like the copper they resemble, seem to draw themselves out, a flutter stretching to search for the source of sound he's now privy to. *Louder,* he says.

Peter, I say. It's his name that escapes me. I let him go on like this for days, hours, or maybe just seconds, until I reach for him, but he's already inside. He has been so for years.

We sit up in the sand in coffee-fresh darkness, as if on the first morning of a long vacation.

"What happened to you?" Peter asks again, points to bruises on my forearm.

"I was going to mule for moolah," I say. But he doesn't understand. "I told a man I'd carry his drugs. I needed money."

He looks at me as if he still doesn't understand. "Hungry mek cat eat salt," I say.

"What happened?"

"I changed my mind."

"Changed your mind?" His eyelids, normally half-mast, fly

open to reveal yellow threads thrashing in the green. I'd never seen his eyes, not really. And he'd never suspected such cliché of me, that I could get involved in the drug trade. Or such recklessness, that I could leave it. I have no explanation. How could I tell him that I thought wrapping myself in cocaine was a good idea, how can one verbalize the abrupt start-up of a Ferris wheel, the nausea of descent after being stuck so long at the top—the need for anaesthetic, stasis.

"It seemed like a good idea. You're the only person that knows." I tell him about Monarch. How he pulled my arm almost from its socket, coveting it for himself.

"I know who he is," he says.

"Really?"

"I think so." He might know exactly who Monarch is. But then again, the pinpoint look that comes from such primordial green could simply be a focus on me.

We lie there on the ground and do not speak. Language will not change the outcome of my excursion. We lie there until he leads me inside.

"We could watch movies," he says.

He puts on Steve McQueen. I fall asleep immediately. I awake later to see Peter watching over me. I drift off again, only to awake beside a half-eaten warmed-over pizza covered with anchovies, my favorite—and Peter, awake like the night. He's turned down the volume on the set, so as not to disturb me. And, except for the crashing of waves in an ongoing erosion of his beach, there is silence.

We go outside to walk the coast, the dogs behind us, the blue ahead. It begins to rain, in an instant, we're soaked. Wind surrounds us in the downpour. Life can't be spent watching movies—or is it? We fall on each other with the urgency of the passing storm. He presses me against his stucco house. We kiss. Water streams over our mouths, a cold to quench. Plaster rubs my paisley, now made visible both by the coming day and far off flashes of lightning that illuminate my skin like a strobe, slowing our movement or so it seems, although we stand racing, one against the other. His shadow of beard is rough on my face, it forces time against me. And so I up my velocity. I reach down for him, slide my tongue in circles around his scar, our scar, the first scar, then lower, envelop his erection. Peter pulls me back up, my mouth to his, sour to salt, and I go down once more. Again, he pulls my mouth to his; I taste anchovies, Malta. Peter strips off his pants, but leaves his shirt on. There's something pedomorphic about this—the curves of buttocks and hamstrings that peek from beneath a sodden t-shirt gives Peter the appearance of a boy-child who has played too long in the rain, and somehow lost his pants.

I press against him in protection. The tank he gave me to replace my sand-covered shift is heavy, its water-laden cotton binds me. Peter lifts it like a curtain. He breathes in my flesh, his mouth open on my unmarked breasts. Rain confuses our borders. Peter cries out. His volume is alarming; it reaches the dogs who've run inside to huddle beneath the kitchen table. Howls swirl again inside me. Outside they begin, barely audible, to surface. He kneads me in rhythm with the rain until he brings forth my battened voice, until I join him in the riot of inarticulation that is the language of longing. He keens short and abrupt, like the splatter of gunfire; my sounds come longer, calling him forth. I lead him gently to the sand, lay him on a pillow of wet garments, then climb atop. Like the last piece of a puzzle our fit gives way to a picture until now unformed— with an ease I can't believe. *Easy ways.* I see in my ecstasy how like disease desire is. Both states can insinuate themselves into a body split-second, as if, perhaps, they'd been there all along. In a hypermnesis of cells, an atavism of salt. I try to stop the state, to freeze up, to feel pain, but I can't. My cells drag me further toward pleasure, acute and unbearable in its brevity. I laugh at such helplessness. His eyes meet mine in a moment's query—then he calls out coming, and I follow, hunched over, my head in his neck, his bottom bucking, our flesh sealing and separating in slaps—like bodies applauding. *Oh Yes Oh Yes.* We cry out together in an antiphony acclaiming our union. Knowing it didn't stand a chance.

Every voyage in life is a foretaste of death. This is how I'd known to travel. In the time we were together, Peter and I made love no less than thrice a day, excursions we could not help taking, each their own reminder of endings.

I saw the way locals began to look at him, and he, valiant, looked toward me—away from his actuality. I knew he wanted children, knew, too, that no matter how much he admired my freedom, he would lock me up—and his home's stucco would crumble as I pounded on its doors.

One day when he told me to meet him after he'd run the boats, I'd stopped in the distance to take in the bevy of women that surrounded him. They were beautiful. They didn't struggle beneath his gaze, but remained immobile, fraught with devotion. And there I stood, back in the distance. So I walked away.

That was the last time I saw him. I spoke once to him on the phone before leaving. "You're going?" he'd echoed.

"Yes," I said.

"Won't you change your mind?"

"No, no."

His voice cracked with tenderness, his pause became lengthy—and because I sensed closure, and because my telephone etiquette was abysmal—I simply hung up. Already I'd heard myself as a memory. So I left for the airport. And that afternoon I flew away, as if I was part of the season's change, as if compelled by solstice.

On my way to change planes in San Juan, I'm stopped by security. I stand back, nervous for no reason, and watch uniformed men with mustaches rifle through my bags. I dig in the batik ink-splotch ruin of my purse, pull up a matchbox and the last of my cigarettes. When I slide the box open with my shaking hand, I find that, but for one match, the box is full of buds. *Shit*. Suddenly I become very calm. Security, with their exhaustive search, would find the pot—and I'd spend the night in a Puerto Rican jail.

I make peace with this kink in my schedule. I have no other plans. Maybe someone will know a good lawyer.

The men finish ripping up my baggage. I lift my arms, a victory V in surrender to be searched; they move me through. My hand is tight around the matchbox, my cigarette unlit. I look around at brethren victims. Security is suspicious, it seems, only of fellow "Latin" types. (Although I could be anything—Arabic, Israeli, or just tan.)

Past the barrier to customs, I light my cigarette. Watch its plume of smoke rise smoothly from fingertips, accelerate toward concrete walls, and splinter into a thousand wild eddies. I watch and, knowing that this is my life, that I'm still in it, and that Chaos is my patron saint—I draw deep.

Acknowledgments

Danella Carter and Eli Gottlieb had the generosity of spirit to guide this book toward print. The faith of my extraordinary agent, Neeti Madan, saw it through. Ramona Lofton's reassurance and wisdom sustained me through the growth of . . . *Girl*, as did the early support of Sharon Sheehe Stark and the kindness and inspiration of Rick Moody. This book also would not have been possible without the courage of Rebecca Koh; the care and confidence of Calvert D. Morgan, Jr.; the recognition of Melissa Jacobs; the Corporation of Yaddo; Donna Brodie and the Writer's Room, NYC.

My deepest thanks to Julie Regan, Robert Polito, David Bornstein, and David Thorpe for their invaluable comments on the manuscript.

For the time and effort it took to ensure your words reached my book along its chaotic journey, my eternal gratitude to all the writers whose praise appears on . . . *Girl*'s jacket. I remain humbled by your generosity.

I am indebted to Dr. Stanley B. Burns for the body of my novel. The marks of the unnamed young woman in his photograph, "Paisley Girl," had a meaning my own scars seemed to lack—in her swirls I saw the mark on Everyperson's skin. Burns's collection of photographs taken by, for, and of the common people is unparalleled in its strength of historic iconic images and images of life's dark side. His " . . . Girl" allowed me to try and give voice to the human condition like no other work could have. I first saw this photograph in *Harm's Way*, by Joel-Peter Witkin (Editor). I've long admired Mr. Witkin's work and am intensely grateful to him as well.

And to Douglas Brinkley, for his belief; Maria Carola for her relentless pursuit of excellence; Jenny Dworkin for her energy and intelligence; Mark Kohut, my hero; Wah-Ming Chang, for artistic insight and careful attention to the text; Robert Wallace; Terese Svoboda, my surrogate sis, for affection, advice, and humor in hard times. Her early reading, along with those of George LaVoo, Dare Dukes, and Deborah Eamon helped speed up a seemingly endless process. I'm grateful for literate companionship of the estimable Sigrid Nunez, Jenifer Berman, Ted Mooney, Sarah Arvio, and Lois Gould; the grace and humanity of Rob Spillman and Elissa Schappell; the patience and generosity of Francine Prose; the poetry of Lilly Dilustro; the moral support of A.M. Homes, N.J. Burkett, Mark Pellington, Josh Miller, and Dorothy Allison. Thank you, William T. Vollmann, for wishing a certain girl could speak. And thank you, Pam Painter. The line *Meanings migrate like lemmings* . . . is Douglas Glover's. Thanks, Doug. Please don't sue me. Thanks also to Charlotte Sheedy, Octavia Wiseman, David Forrer, Chris Noël, Leslie Lee, O. Aldon James (champion of artists), Marian Sumner, Jeff Hogan and Cultural Exhaust, The Waghorns, Anne Greene and the Wesleyan Writer's Conference, Glenville Lovell; my family and friends, too numerous to mention. For all, my greatest thanks.